a Secret harvest

Dave Webber

a Secret harvest

Dave Webber

Wrate's Publishing

Wrate's Publishing

a secret harvest

First published 2018 by Wrate's Publishing

ISBN 978-1-9996089-3-4

Edited and typeset by Wrate's Editing Services
www.wrateseditingservices.co.uk

A CIP catalogue record for this book is available from the British Library.

Printed and bound by CPI Group (UK) Ltd, Croydon, CRO 4YY

*To Anni, for her patience, inspiration,
love and constant encouragement.*

Chapter One

A Rude Awakening

At 6am, Tom Dwyer opened his eyes and quickly closed them again. He buried his head in the pillow, hoping that his brain wouldn't notice he was awake and allow him to sleep a little longer. But old habits die hard, and they would not let him rest. He looked around the small and rather shabby room that he had known for almost forty years, before eventually forcing himself to kick back the blankets and pull on some clothes. He stumbled down the stairs to the bathroom to wash.

Although the late summer's day was already bright and the sun was beginning to show through a small window, the water struck icy cold. Tom thought how nice it would be if it was warm, but Dad could never be convinced that such things were necessary. He would never agree to anything that was about making life more comfortable. It was as though he felt he didn't deserve it. On several occasions, Tom had made suggestions about improving their living arrangements, but these were quickly dismissed. The result was always the same – they would argue and Dad would become upset and distressed. Tom ended up dropping the matter. Only recently, when Dad got sick, Tom suggested buying him a new bed. He was quite ready to pay, but Dad got so angry that it was not spoken about again.

For today, Tom reconciled himself to the cold and continued with his ablutions. As he finished dressing, he rebuked himself. *If you want hot water, Tom Dwyer, then there's no reason in the world why you shouldn't have it, so stop worrying about what Dad might say!*

The morning passed in the way that mornings always did when Tom didn't have to work. That is to say, half in boredom and half in doing anything that might stop him thinking about work. He wished that he were immersed in his well-established daily routine; somehow he felt safe at work. At home by himself, he felt exposed and guilty, like a child playing hooky from school. Worst of all, he was lethargic and at a loose end. He made a mental note to himself. *One more day and I'm off back to work, no matter what anyone says.*

On this particular morning, that sense of being exposed and without purpose was even stronger. He busied himself, needlessly hoeing the carrot bed by lightly turning the dry, lighter topsoil into the damp, darker earth. It was satisfying. You could see exactly what you had done; you could see exactly where you had left your mark. As he worked, Tom thought about his life in general. Could he see where he had left his mark? What had he done? Not much was his conclusion, which made him feel even more miserable.

Tom looked at his watch; it was 8:30 – time to go and get Dad's breakfast. He was removing the loose soil from his boots by stamping them on the concrete path when he was brought up short by a cold sensation that turned to anger. *He's bloody gone – can't you understand that? It's been over two bloody weeks and you still can't get that into your thick head!*

He sat on the garden seat and watched as a robin took up a classic pose on the handle of the garden fork. Tom was sweating, his head was sore and he felt nauseous. Clouds had obscured the sun and a light rain was beginning to fall, so he went indoors. He decided that some food might help him to feel a little better, but the remaining bread was displaying a pale green mould and the eggs were older than he could remember. He cleared it all into the bin and settled on cereal, but there was no milk! Tom sat for a while in the dingy kitchen. Then he caught himself. *You're wallowing again, Tom Dwyer. Pull yourself together!*

He began to clear up the small kitchen. As he tidied, he found a half-empty rum bottle, which told the story of the day before and explained the way he was now feeling. Tom had never been much of a drinker, but this week it had provided just what he needed. But enough was enough. *Today is the day I stop wallowing and get on,* he told himself.

He emptied the overflowing bin, put on the kettle for washing up and went upstairs to grab a clean shirt.

The feeling of loneliness and isolation was almost too much to bear. For years, there had been no real friends in Tom's life and Dad had long since made it clear that visitors to the house weren't welcome. Consequently, when Dad died, no one came to visit except Tom's employers, Jack and Laura Deacon. All in all, work was the only real contact Tom had with other people.

He was making inroads into the high stack of washing up when a sharp knock on the front door seemed to reverberate on every surface of the cottage. It shook him to his bones and he almost jumped out of his skin. Throwing the dishcloth into the washing up bowl, he hurried out of the back door, into the garden, and around to the front one, which had not been opened for years. He dried his hands on his trousers as he went.

"Mr Dwyer?" A smartly dressed young man held out his hand.

Tom did not take it; he was suspicious and thought he was probably selling something. "That's me," he said abruptly and, realising his shortness, corrected himself. "Erm, what can I do for you?"

"Mr Dwyer, I'm Martin Stone of Stone, Blackman and Co Solicitors. We were getting concerned that you hadn't responded to our letter."

"Letter?" said Tom. "I haven't seen a letter."

The two men stood looking at each other with puzzled expressions.

"Hang on," said Tom. He hurried up the garden towards the front gate, where there was a wooden mailbox on a pole. He opened the back and removed two letters.

"Well, there's a thing," he said to his visitor. "Dad always fetched the letters. I'd totally forgotten about them. We only get the odd bill from time to time."

Opening the long, white envelope, Tom saw that the letter bore the heading of Stone, Blackman & Co.

Dear Mr Dwyer,

We were very sorry to learn of the death of your father, Mr J W Dwyer, and we would like to take this opportunity to extend our condolences to you at this time.

As you may be aware, your father has instructed us in certain matters, in relation to his estate, which in the event of his death require us to take certain actions. In order for us to put these matters in hand, would you please contact us at your earliest convenience to discuss in more detail your late father's estate.

Yours sincerely,

Martin Stone, LLB

Tom stared at the letter, not knowing what to think. Estate – what estate? Dad didn't own anything other than the cottage, and that had been transferred into the joint names of Tom and his sister, Ella, about ten years ago, not long before she died.

Realising that they had been standing unceremoniously in the garden, he spoke up. "Err, I'm sorry. Would you like to come in?"

As they walked into the rather dark kitchen, Tom apologised for the unfinished washing up, grabbed some clothes from a chair and offered his guest a seat.

"I am rather confused to be honest," he said. "I can't think what estate there is to discuss."

Martin Stone opened his briefcase. "OK, let's see what we can do to help you. To be frank, things are not that clear to me, either, as my own father, who has dealt with this case up to now, has just undergone heart surgery and is completely out of the picture. I'm therefore learning, too. Firstly, you should know that his estate falls entirely to you."

"Yes, I knew that. There was about £5,500 in cash in a box. He always kept it under his bed. I paid the funeral director and the rest is still there."

"No, Mr Dwyer, there is rather more than that. I mean, the property alone..." Stone broke off as he saw the realisation on Tom's face.

"Ah, yes, I know the cottage is now mine – that was signed over years ago."

"Absolutely, but surely you must be aware that your father's estate amounts to substantially more than this cottage?"

"In what way?"

Stone clocked the bemusement return to Tom's face and realised that this may not be as straightforward as he had initially thought. "Well, to begin with, there's Glebe Farm and Larkspur House."

Tom stared at Stone in a way that showed his suspicion and distrust. "What is this? What do you mean?"

"I mean," said Stone, with supreme patience, "that the tenant at Larkspur is very concerned about how your father's death will affect her tenure."

"Well, why should it affect her?" Tom was indignant and Stone's patience was now giving way to frustration.

"Mr Dwyer, there seems to be some misunderstanding. You are the new landlord of Larkspur and Glebe Farm. You own both the house and the farmland. In fact, the entire estate."

Tom tried to interrupt, but Stone went on. "Your father was letting both on a peppercorn rent."

Tom got up from the table and went to stand at the window. He was visibly shaking. "Look, this is all a big mistake. Mrs Margesson owns Larkspur House and Glebe Farm. That estate has not been mentioned in this house for twenty years, not since Dad worked there."

Stone was shocked that Tom really didn't appear to know anything about his father's affairs; he could not imagine what that must feel like. "Mr Dwyer, Mrs Margesson died some years ago. She left Larkspur House and Glebe Farm, as well as her substantial business interests, to your father."

"That's rubbish," said Tom.

"I am afraid it is not. Your father allowed Mrs Margesson's granddaughter, Miss Aldridge, to stay on in the house at a peppercorn rent. Her daughter and her son-in-law were killed in a car accident many years ago. Miss Aldridge also holds the lease to Glebe Farm, which she sublets to Jack Deacon. He's a farmer."

"Yes, I know perfectly well who Jack Deacon is," Tom said. "He happens to be my employer."

The sheer absurdity of what was happening was beginning to irritate him. Tom had always worked for the Deacons. He was now manager of their mixed, 600-acre farm, about a quarter of a mile away.

Stone realised how difficult this was going to be. "I'm not sure why your father didn't tell you," he said, "but you are now a wealthy man, Tom. The fact is that Larkspur House and Glebe Farm are only the tip of the iceberg. There is substantially more, but I've not managed to get a complete picture yet." He handed Tom a piece of folded paper. "This is a copy of your father's last will and testament. As you can see, it was signed and dated by him just two months ago, when he last visited our office. Would you like me to read through it?"

Tom felt cold inside, and that culminated in a sensation he knew as fear. "No, I'll read it," he said, holding out his hand.

"There's money on deposit at Western Shires Building Society, and we hold the key to a safety deposit box at Lloyds Bank in Downfield, where there is a current account." Stone could see that Tom had already heard more than he could take in. “Look,” he added, “you need some time to absorb all of this. Could you have a read through and come into our offices tomorrow. Any time after 2pm?”

“OK,” said Tom, “I think I can do that.”

“Now, is there anything else you’d like to know for now?”

“No, I’d better read this,” Tom replied, holding up the will. His voice was weak and he was preoccupied with his thoughts.

“OK, fine. We can deal with any questions you have tomorrow. But don’t worry, we will be with you every step of the way.”

Tom understood that many people would be really excited if they had just come into money, but he knew himself – he knew that he would remain cautious until he comprehended all of the story’s upsides and downsides.

As Tom closed the door behind Stone, his head spun as he tried to process what he had just heard. Thoughts were tumbling over and over in his mind. He slumped into the old armchair in the kitchen and read the document several times over. It restated everything Stone had said, and although it held very few actual figures, it was obvious that the estate was very substantial indeed. Tom knew that he couldn’t avoid dealing with it, but there was still so much he didn’t understand. He had never been in possession of much money, but he could see that with it came some serious responsibilities. He knew there would be things like death duties and costs tied up with property ownership. His natural cautiousness would not let him think about the potential upside to the situation. Tom also wondered why the money had not been kept in the Margesson family? How must they feel? He went to bed that night with all of these questions dominating his thoughts, which made for a very restless night's sleep.

The following day, as Tom got off the bus in Downfield, the Town Hall clock struck 1pm. He realised he was too early. It was hard to judge the timing. His village was only eight miles from Downfield, but the service bus called at six others before completing its journey, so the route took over an hour in total. As he aimlessly wandered up and down the high street, he spotted a small café and stepped inside. Only one other customer was present, and he was reading the newspaper.

"Hello, love, sit down. What can I get you?" a woman in a brightly coloured overall said from behind the counter.

"I'll have a tea, please, and a ham sandwich," Tom replied.

"OK, dear. What a lovely morning it's been, hasn't it? I was just saying to Bob over there how well we've done for summer this year."

"Err, yes we have."

The woman continued to chat, but Tom wasn't really taking it in. As he ate his sandwich and drank his tea, he gazed through the net curtains at the offices of Stone, Blackman & Co opposite. He saw a woman of about forty or so coming out of the building and down the steps to the street. He thought he might know her, but he couldn't quite place her face. Though her shock of auburn curls was very familiar. Now, where had he seen them before? He kept his eyes on her as she wandered off down the high street before disappearing out of view. Tom finished his sandwich and paid his bill. The woman behind the counter called to him,

"You have a nice day, love!" as he closed the door behind him.

Chapter Two

Father and Son

Although the exterior of the solicitor's office was old and formal, the interior took Tom by surprise. Big, soft leather armchairs were set around a large, glass coffee table in the reception area, and a young woman was seated at a heavy looking glass and stainless steel desk.

"Good afternoon, sir, may I help you?"

"Yes, please," said Tom. "My solicitor is, err, Mr Stone."

"Yes, sir, would that be Mr Martin Stone?

"Err, I think so."

"Well, there are two, but Mr William Stone is not in the office for a week or so."

"Oh, yes, then it must be," said Tom. "I'm sorry, I'd forgotten there were two."

"I'll check that he is free for you, sir. Your name is...?"

"Dwyer," said Tom.

"Ah, yes, of course, Mr Dwyer. I know he is expecting you. Just one moment."

Tom was shaking again. He swallowed hard and took a deep breath in order to steady himself.

The woman returned. "He'll just be a couple of moments. Would you like to take a seat?"

Tom stooped to sit in one of the easy chairs, but he stopped short and walked to the window instead. Looking out onto the main street, he watched the people of Downfield going about their business. He realised that all of this went on every day, without him even knowing. He felt slightly resentful that life should carry on so normally when his own was in such chaos. A voice from behind him made him jump, and he turned to see Martin Stone extending a hand. "Hello, Tom, thanks for coming in – would you like to come through?"

He led Tom down a small corridor and into a large, well-appointed office. Offering him a large, red leather chair next to his desk, he took his own seat behind it and opened a thick, pink file. "I'm sorry that yesterday was such a shock. I had no idea your father had not discussed anything with you."

"Dad never said a thing about any of this," said Tom, "as far as I knew, he had nothing other than what was in the house."

Tom's anxiety was starting to get the better of him again. "The point is, I don't know anything about property and leases, etc., and I am worried I won't be able to afford repairs on a place as large as Larkspur House. I may just have to get rid of it."

"Tom, you will have no problems with money, and we can give you all the advice and guidance you need. Besides, it's let on a fully maintained lease, which means the repairs, other than the roof and walls, are the responsibility of the tenant. Before you think about selling, you should give yourself some time to think, or at least wait until we know what the estate amounts to in full. I've drawn up a list of the obvious assets, although before we can be sure what the final amount will be, we will, of course, have to wait for the Revenue to do its calculations in relation to death duty."

"Yes, I've been worried about that. I've read about it almost ruining people. I don't want to lose the cottage."

"Tom," said Stone patiently. "You will not lose anything. You are a wealthy man. All we have to do is take stock of the whole estate so that we can get things cleared up as soon as possible. Now, that's where I need your help. I've established that there is £120,000 invested with Western Shires Building Society."

Tom took a sharp intake of breath and almost smiled, but, once again, his natural caution kicked in. He couldn't process good news until he fully understood it.

Stone continued. "There is also a substantial sum of money on account with Lloyds. I've asked the manager to calculate this and prepare a statement, which will be ready for us this afternoon. I also have a key for a safety deposit box, with instructions that it must be passed to you in such circumstances as these. The box is at Lloyds and you should take a look at it soon to establish whether there is anything in there that needs to be dealt with, such as papers relating to money or shares, either in the box or at home. It would be best if they could then be handed to me. I am particularly keen to find lease papers for Larkspur. I would be happy to come with you to the bank now, if you wish, or we can fix another time. Of course, you may prefer to go on your own?"

"No," said Tom. "I really wouldn't know where to start. If you could come with me, I'd be very glad."

The two men left the office and walked down the street in silence. Tom was feeling anxious as he tried to work through the thoughts going on inside his head. He thought about the £120,000 and couldn't help feeling a little excited.

Stone introduced Tom to the branch manager, and he escorted the two visitors to a small, private room in which two staff members produced a very large, tin box. Stone pushed the key into the lock and the lid opened without any trouble to reveal a selection of envelopes. There was also a small, brown leather case. Stone removed a pad from his briefcase and opened the first envelope. "These are the lease agreements and title deeds to Glebe Farm," he said, making a note of them. "I'm glad we've found them."

A large pile of loose papers followed, along with a bundle of pink, blue and green envelopes, some of which had the familiar red and blue border that once signified airmail. The envelopes had been carefully tied together and Tom released the bow that held them in place and laid them on the table. Most of the envelopes were handwritten in careful writing that he did not recognise, and each one was addressed to Mr John Dwyer c/o Stone, Blackman & Co. At the bottom of the pile were a few letters written in a bold, meticulous hand, which he knew to belong to his father. He looked briefly at a couple of them and realised they were personal exchanges between his dad and Emily Margesson. He knew that he should probably read them as they may help him to understand what had happened a little better, but this was not the place to do it.

"Could I take these with me?" he asked Stone.

"Yes, of course, Tom."

"What are those?" he asked, pointing to a thick pile of papers that Stone was working through.

"Mostly share certificates," Stone replied. He was sifting through them and making notes as he went. "This one is addressed to you," he said, removing the next envelope. Tom took it and once again recognised his father's meticulous handwriting.

He tore open the envelope and began to read...

My Dear Tom,

If you are reading this, then it means that I am either dead or no longer fit to manage my own affairs. I know that you'll be confused and probably angry with me, and I don't blame you for that.

Tom, there have been many things in my life that I'm not proud of and some are so painful that I was not able to bring myself to discuss them with you, as I know I should have done. For that I realise I am an awful coward and have let you down.

Your mother and I both managed to hurt each other, but despite the turmoil in our lives she chose to stay with us until you and Ella were of an age to deal with her leaving. She then went off to find a new life, and I hope it's been a happy one. Please try not to judge her – she stayed longer than could reasonably have been expected. Please do try to believe me when I say that she loved you both and had good reason for going.

I hope that by now you will have found love and understand its power. If not, may you do so soon. In my view, it's the very reason for life and therefore the cause of so many of our trials and much of our happiness. I am afraid I missed my chance to be with the love of my life, and all I can say is to take your chances as they come, Tom – some only come once.

You will begin to understand, son, and I know you will be just fine. Trust Mr Stone, he's been a friend and a good support to me through some very rough times. Once again, I'm sorry I couldn't have done things better.

God bless you,

Dad

Tom read quickly, only scanning the words, as he did not want to take in what he was faced with. So many things were racing through his mind about his past life and he began to sweat. It seemed like there were rocks in his stomach, churning over and over. He couldn't read anymore. Tears filled his eyes and his throat was dry and painful. He pushed the letter towards Stone, who was about to open the leather case. "I can't do this," he said. "I need time to take it all in."

Stone read the letter and then pushed open the lid of the case, which was purpose designed for jewellery. It contained necklaces, rings and bracelets. Tom had never seen them before.

"Some beautiful pieces here," Stone commented. He held up a Rolex Oyster watch and Tom took it from him. He remembered its rather ornate face, with a crown under the number twelve. He'd studied it so many times back when it was on his father's wrist. He remembered watching it tick as his dad worked to balance the accounts or make up the men's wages. That watch had been on the wrist that had played cricket with him as a boy and pushed Ella on the swing in the garden of their first home. Happy times.

"I never realised this old thing was still around, but I've never seen any of the other stuff in my life!"

"Well, they belong to you now," said Stone, trying to take control of the situation.

"None of this is making any sense to me, Mr Stone. At the moment it feels like a bad dream. I need some time to decide what to do."

"Of course," said Stone, "it's going to take me a while to list this lot, too, but it has to be done. I know this is very hard for you, but certain matters like Larkspur House cannot be ignored for long. Miss Aldridge came to see me this morning. She is very worried, so we must get that tied up. I need to read the lease documents and find out for you how we stand."

"Yes," Tom agreed. "We have to get this mess sorted out, but for now, if she's worried, please just tell her things will stay as they are."

"OK," said Stone, "but there's no reason why you should continue this kind of goodwill arrangement on such a valuable property. But for now I think we've probably done enough for one day. I suggest that we leave the valuables here and transfer the paperwork to my office. I'll go through it and let you have a list of what's there."

"Good," said Tom, "that would be better. You're right – I have had enough."

Stone returned the jewellery to the box, along with a bag of coins. As he reached for the Rolex, Tom asked, "Can I hold on to that?"

"I don't see why not, it can't really hurt," said Stone, as he packed the remaining papers into his briefcase.

By now it was 4:30pm and Downfield was beginning to close for the day. Stone was headed back to his office.

"Let's catch up in a day or so. How about Wednesday afternoon at two?"

"Fine," said Tom. "I'll be there."

It was almost six when Tom arrived home. The birds were singing their final chorus before starting to settle for the night. The sun was still shining as he sat on a bench in the garden and sipped a mug of tea. He loved this time of year; everything was green and lush and the garden looked well ordered.

He was brought to his senses by the sound of a car pulling up in the road beyond the hedge. He took little notice, as it was common for people to stop there in order to run their dogs in the field opposite. But then the tall, broad form of George Deacon appeared at the gate and fumbled at the latch. "Good evening, Tom!" he said in his usual jovial tone. "We thought it was time to see how you were doing."

"Oh, that's nice of you, boss," said Tom, getting to his feet and feeling very guilty that he'd not been in touch since the funeral. It seemed strange to Tom to see his boss at the cottage. "I'm doing OK, thanks, but to tell you the truth I've still got one hell of a mess to sort out, so I think I need a few more days yet."

"That's fine, Tom, just do what you need to do, and don't worry, you have never taken a holiday and Frank has the harvest well under control – he doesn't organise the men as well as you, but I'm keeping an eye on him and there are no real problems. To tell you the truth, it will would do him good."

Tom stared at the garden, a distant look in his eye. As he didn't speak, George felt compelled to break the silence. "Look, Tom, if you need help sorting things out..."

"Thanks, boss, but I've got a lot to get straight before it will make any sense to anyone else. It appears that Dad's affairs are a lot more complicated than I thought. You know, legal stuff."

"Alright, but if you need anything, just let me know. Have you got a good solicitor?"

"I think so," said Tom, "Stone, Blackman and Co."

George smiled his approval. "They have been my solicitors for years, they'll see you right."

Once again, Tom felt a pang of guilt as he remembered that the Glebe land was now his and sublet to George. But he was not yet ready to say anything about it.

"Why don't you drop by and see Laura over the next day or so? She's been asking after you – she'd love to see you."

"I will," said Tom. "How is she?"

"Pretty good, but that damned arthritis doesn't let her go too far on her pins."

After George had gone, Tom sat alone in the kitchen, going over the events of the day. Remembering the Rolex watch, he took it from his jacket pocket. Turning the winder, it began to mark the passing of time at once. Tom put it right by the kitchen clock, though he was not hopeful it would continue to work – it was dirty and the face was scratched, but he remembered it oh so well.

He spent the rest of the evening immersed in reading the letters between his father and Emily Margesson. He couldn't deny that they were really quite moving. His father's rather flamboyant but neat writing expressed such feeling in a language that Tom struggled to imagine him ever using. These were clearly happy times for the young John Dwyer. It seemed that the early letters had been returned to John along with Emily's replies, presumably to prevent them from being found. Emily's letters also expressed great feelings of love. Tom noticed that the dates on them spanned decades.

It was only when he heard the clock on the wall strike midnight that he tied the letters back into their bundle and went to bed. With memories of the past drifting through his mind, he fell into a deep sleep.

By 9:30 the next morning, Tom had already been to the village shop and was sitting down to boiled eggs. It felt strange to be wearing the watch, as he'd never been allowed to touch it as a child. It was still keeping perfect time. After breakfast, Tom remembered that Martin Stone had asked him to look at home for any relevant papers or deeds. He really didn't think there was anything in the house, but he decided to have a look anyway, beginning his search in the most likely place – the old bureau in the sitting room. It gave up no immediate secrets, but Tom made a mental note that it needed clearing. He looked around the room, which was hardly ever used – everything had gathered dust. Most of the furniture was too big for the room, but had been brought here by his parents from their first home. The books that lined the shelves had remained untouched for years; the piano unplayed since Ella last played Für Elise. The sheet music she used remained on display almost as a memorial to her. This room was never a comfortable place for Tom and it had always felt more like a museum than part of his home.

He returned to the kitchen, taking an address book from the desk. He made some tea and began to flick through the yellowing pages. He'd looked through this book just after his dad died, trying to find a reference to his uncle – his dad's younger brother. The family hadn't been close and

Al, short for Albert, hadn't been seen or heard of by Tom for many years. The other addresses, some foreign, meant nothing to him. At the back of the book, several scraps of paper had been folded and it was here that Tom found the address of Stone, Blackman & Co, as well as Lloyds Bank in Downfield. There was also an address he could not explain – it simply said 'Castillion' PO Box 206 Sausalito, California. Tom had never heard of it, but he felt ready to get more information now and wished that he'd asked more questions when he was with Stone. The £120,000 came into his mind again and he began to contemplate what he might do with some of it; that is if there was any left after tax and solicitor's fees, and suchlike. *There could be a bit left, though,* he said to himself with a smile.

Chapter Three

An Alpha Male

Once again, Tom felt strange as he sat in the unfamiliar environment of the solicitor's office waiting room. So much had happened over the last few days and he was still struggling to make sense of it all. He hoped that this meeting would help to make things clearer. Clutched tight in his hand was the bundle of envelopes that he had taken from the safety deposit box. He had read each of the letters they held several times over and felt it would be best if they were returned to safe keeping, which would prevent any of the information in them getting out. He had thought about burning them but decided against it. Eventually, he found himself sitting opposite Martin Stone, who was so far the only person who seemed to understand the situation he was in.

"How are you, Tom, how does it all feel?" he asked in a rather matter-of-fact manner. "Miss Aldridge is not due for another half an hour. I thought you and I might need to talk before she arrives." Stone knew that Tom was still far from comfortable with the situation. "Have you read the letters?"

"Yes," said Tom. "And they have not made things much better. I thought I knew my father and all of this just goes to prove that I didn't. When I buried him a few weeks ago, I thought that was it. My life was simple and I could see where I was going, but now?" Tom handed Stone the letters and asked him to put them somewhere secure.

"Do we need to talk about what's in them?" Stone asked.

"No," replied Tom. "It's all straightforward enough. My father obviously continued a relationship with Emily Margesson right up until her death."

Stone picked up the somewhat resentful tone in Tom's voice. "I know how tough this is for you," he said. "It must be very painful, but it will get better."

"Yes," said Tom. "I know it will, but I need to get all of the information I can. It might help me make sense of it, though it doesn't seem likely. I am a straightforward man, Mr Stone, and I have no idea where to go or who to trust with all of this. The money is a huge worry, and it still feels like it's not really mine and that this is all a huge mistake."

"Look, Tom," said Stone, trying to move things along. "I have asked Miss Aldridge here today because you have joint business interests now and you need to meet and discuss them. In terms of the estate as a whole, I have prepared a statement of the position as I see it, based on what we know at the moment, although we need to get accountants involved to get down to details. A broker urgently needs to be consulted about the shares. I will look into asking Baverstock and Lyle, they were your father's accountants. There are a lot of investments involved here and I am not qualified to advise you on those. But for today there is urgent business to resolve about Larkspur, Glebe Farm and Margesson Holdings. Some arrangements for the immediate future need to be made."

"I'm not sure that I am ready to deal with all of that. Can

you sort it out for me? I don't think I want to meet Miss Aldridge."

"Yes, it could be done that way if that is what you really want, but it would be much easier and quicker in the long run if we could get around a table, at least to start with – and you did agree to meet her, Tom. She is finding this very difficult, too. I thought it would be simpler all round if the pair of you could talk."

"I suppose so," Tom replied, "but I don't know what I am going to say to her. I will leave it to you to let me know."

At that moment, Stone's secretary put her head around the door. "Excuse me, Mr Stone, but Miss Aldridge and Mr Dyson are here. I know they are early, but I thought you would like to know."

"Thanks, Eileen. Are you OK, Tom?"

"I suppose so."

"Show her into the conference room, Eileen, will you, please?" He turned to Tom. "When you are ready," he said, and the two men got up together.

"Who is Dyson?" Tom asked, sounding anxious.

Stone cast his eyes upwards. "He is Miss Aldridge's friend and advisor," he explained. "He is a bit tricky to be honest, but I will deal with him."

As they entered the conference room, two people were already seated at the table. Tom recognised one as the red-haired woman he had seen leaving this very office a few days ago, when he was sitting in the café. The other was a smartly dressed young man of average build. He was wearing a three-piece suite and had already spread a load of papers out on the table. He was currently busying himself with straightening his hair in the mirror. They sat down and Stone began. "Thank you all for agreeing to come today. I thought this meeting would be a good idea in order to settle a few things. This is Mr Dwyer – he is the new owner of Larkspur House and Glebe Farm. He also owns a twenty per cent share of Margesson Holdings. Mr Dwyer and I have discussed the current situation with Larkspur and Glebe Farm and I am instructed to tell you that we will hold present charges and conditions for six months."

"But what happens then?" asked Dyson.

"We don't know, but we will have options. We may choose to renew on current terms, or we may decide to make a fair and proper valuation for market rent, or, depending on Mr Dwyer's decision in the meantime, the property could go on the market for sale."

"You can't do that!" said Dyson – his cut-glass accent giving him a superior air – "Not without giving us proper notice."

"If that is the course we decide to take, we will serve the appropriate notice according to the law," said Stone.

"What do you mean 'if'?" said Dyson. "You know full well that you have already made your mind up to sell and get your hands on the money." He glared at Tom. "And as for Glebe Farm, well, they are behind on their rent and owe us money, so we may well be starting legal proceedings there. Don't get your hopes up about a big income from that."

Tom was shocked to hear that Jack was in debt, but he chose not to say anything.

"Mr Dyson," said Stone, shaking his head. "You are wrong. No one has decided anything. I am simply making you aware of the possibilities. We also need to discuss the future running of Margesson Holdings; my client is now a substantial shareholder."

"Now look," replied Dyson, in a patronising manner. "Margesson Holdings has been in some difficulty for a while, and it's only just getting back on an even keel, so don't think there is any great fortune to be had from it. Just tell me how much you would like for your shares and I will see what we can do – they are not worth much, but I can see you would rather be without the responsibility."

Anna Aldridge sat quietly with her hands tightly clenched and her eyes on the floor. On occasion, she frowned.

Dyson continued. "It's only thanks to my taking things over that we did not go down a year ago. You are going to take away Anna's home, that's bad enough, but I can't have you meddling in the business as well." He turned to face Tom, who was blushing from rising anger. "Your family has done well enough out of us, Mr Dwyer. Because your father managed to hoodwink a frail old lady, Anna has been left with almost nothing. Why can't you just be satisfied with what you already have and leave us alone?"

Tom drew back in his chair, as Stone stepped in. "Now, Mr Dyson, no one is trying to take anything that isn't theirs under the law. Until a few days ago, Mr Dwyer didn't know anything about his inheritance or even that there was anything to inherit."

"You don't really expect us to believe that?" Dyson replied.

"It's true," said Tom. "I had no idea that my father owned anything other than our house."

Anna looked at Tom and smiled gently, but she did not speak. Stone raised himself up in his chair. "I did understand that you were going to bring your accountant to this meeting, Miss Aldridge?"

Dyson spoke before Anna could answer. "There was no need, I deal with those matters for Anna."

"But you do have an accountant, Miss Aldridge?" Stone persisted.

"You know fine well she does," said Dyson, once again preventing Anna from speaking for herself. "But you can conduct your correspondence through me for now."

"Is that your wish, Miss Aldridge?" Stone asked, looking directly at Anna.

Dyson nodded vigorously, prompting Anna's reply. "Yes, if that's what Alex thinks is best," she said.

"OK, that's fine, then – we will start by asking about the next board meeting," said Stone.

"We don't have one planned as yet," said Dyson.

"Well, we need to ensure that Mr Dwyer or his representative is included in it, and we need copies of the minutes from the last meeting, please."

"Look," said Dyson, once again addressing Tom directly. "No one from your side has been interested up until now, and you weren't bothered about helping when the company was down, so don't think you can come along and start muscling in now..."

"No one is asking for anything other than their rights," Stone interrupted. "My client is entitled to representation on the board and to copies of all the minutes and decisions."

"Put that request in writing"

"Very well, but you know that it's a legal requirement. That is why I asked for your company accountant to be present. I had hoped to get all of this sorted out without these obstructions." Stone was becoming irritated.

"We are not going to be pushed," said Dyson.

"I understand that," Stone replied, "but there is business to be settled and I need to ensure that my client's interests are properly protected. Mr Dwyer does not want to upset anything, but nevertheless, he needs to consolidate his affairs so that he is able to fully understand his position."

"Understand his position?" Dyson mocked. "His position is very clear to me. He stays away until now, won't help when the business is in difficulty and then when it starts to make money wants to realise his investment." He stood up. "Come on, Anna, I've had enough of this. I knew there was no intention to be reasonable. Let's go."

As Anna reached for her coat, Dyson started to pack up his papers.

Meanwhile, Tom had listened for long enough. "Look!" he shouted. "I don't know what all this is about, but I do know that you're not listening. Mr Stone has already told you that I didn't even know about all of this until the other day, so don't keep shouting like I am trying to do you out of something." He turned to Anna. "I am sorry about this, miss, and I will be guided by Mr Stone about what is best. But please don't worry, I will see to it that you're treated fairly and won't put you out of your home if I can."

Anna smiled, but she was quickly ushered out of the room by Dyson. In reception, Eileen got up from her desk to show them out.

"I am really sorry, Tom," Stone said once they were alone. "I had no idea it was going to work out like that. I spoke to Miss Margesson, who was quite willing to come with her accountant, but she called back and told Eileen that he would be coming instead."

Tom was still shaking. "What an awful, awful man."

"Look, Tom, once it's all sorted you don't have to be

involved if you don't want to be. Your father used a firm of accountants and brokers called Baverstock and Lyle from London. We need to meet with them as soon as possible – I'll get Eileen to arrange something."

"OK," said Tom. "But can we assure Miss Aldridge that I am not going to turn her out of house and home?"

Stone sighed. "I think we have said as much as we can, but I will try again tomorrow if that is what you would like." He picked up a folder from his desk. "Here is the breakdown of the contents of the box, as far as I have it at the moment. We are talking about a lot of money here. Right now, it looks like several million pounds and that is without the investments being calculated properly or the property being valued by today's market."

"What am I going to do?" Tom asked.

"Don't worry, we will get this sorted. You need to start thinking about yourself and what you want to do."

"I want things to go back to the way they were," said Tom. "And I need to go back to work. Mr Deacon has been very good, but I can't leave him in the lurch. I don't know how I will face him knowing that I own his farm."

"You should talk to him, Tom," Stone advised. "Would you like me to be with you when you do that?"

"No, thank you. I owe it to Jack and Laura to tell them straight."

"Do you need any money now, or are you OK?"

"I have cash in the house and Mr Deacon is still paying me, so I don't need any more at this point, but thank you."

"Well, if you need to, you can always get some from your current account at the bank – they told me this morning that you now have access in order to meet your immediate expenses, but I am afraid it will be harder to get any large sums until we get probate and the tax sorted out. You could do with setting up an account of your own, as now you will have a monthly director's salary from Margesson Holdings. I will get Eileen onto that for you. Now, how are you getting home? Shall I ask Eileen to send for a cab?"

"I came on the bus," said Tom, "but it would be nice not to have to go back out into that." – He pointed at the window where hard rain was bouncing on the windowsill. – "You need to send me a bill," he added. "I must owe you a fortune by now."

"Don't worry," said Stone after speaking to Eileen on the internal phone. "We will get to that in time."

"Yes, but I don't like owing money." Tom got up and started to put on his coat.

"I will call over and see you the day after tomorrow. Is the afternoon OK?"

Before Tom could reply, Eileen announced the arrival of his taxi. As he got into the vehicle, the driver checked where he wanted to go and pulled away. "The traffic is awful this afternoon," he told Tom. "The weather is flooding the bottom of the High Street and it's all down to one lane."

They made slow progress, and, as Tom looked out of the window, he saw Dyson and Anna Aldridge coming out of the bank. Dyson was guiding her by the arm in a controlling fashion. He then helped her into the passenger seat of an expensive-looking sports car. Tom watched as he slammed the door after her and swaggered round to the driver's side before pushing his way into the traffic going in the opposite direction. As they drove past, Tom decided he disliked Dyson even more than he had in Stone's office.

Chapter Four

Friends in Need

The late afternoon saw the rainstorms breaking and sunlight flooding the garden, which served as a reminder that summer had not completely taken its leave. Although the day had done little to help unravel the mysteries of his situation, Tom was clear what he should do next and he set off with a purposeful step and a determination to face up to one of his responsibilities.

As he walked through the yard at Glebe Farm, he wondered what he was going to say, but Jack was a good friend as well as his employer, and he knew that although he would be shocked, he could trust him to give wise counsel.

Laura Deacon greeted him as he knocked and entered the kitchen. Throughout his working life, Tom had entered this room several times a day, but today everything felt different. Laura was genuinely pleased to see him; her broad smile was warm and made the whole room feel comfortable again. "Tom! How are you?" she said, not leaving him time to answer. "I'll bet you haven't been eating properly, have you? And you are looking tired, too. I hope you'll stay and have some dinner with us?"

Tom was about to decline, but once again, Laura interjected. "Jack's out, but he'll be back in about half an hour for his dinner. Here, what am I thinking? Sit down and let me get you some tea."

Tom did as instructed. When it came to Laura, he was used to not getting a word in edgeways. She was well known in the village as a force to be reckoned with. The forthright sort, she didn't suffer fools and knew almost all there was to know about the village and its residents. While she heard all there was to hear, she never dealt in gossip. Whenever someone needed help, Laura didn't dole out advice but was there in the thick of it, her sleeves rolled up.

Laura returned to the table with tea. "Now then, where have you been hiding yourself? I've not seen you around the village. I was worried that you were shutting yourself away, so I came to see you, but you were out and about somewhere."

Tom took a sip of the dark, strong, sweet tea. He never made tea like this at home. In fact, he preferred it weak, with only a little sugar, but tea had always been this way at Glebe Farm and it felt familiar and safe. "Sorry," he said. "I've been back and forth to Downfield, sorting things out with solicitors and banks and all that. I haven't been in all that much."

"Is it all sorted out now?" Laura asked.

"Not really," said Tom, "that's why I wanted to talk to you and the boss."

"I'm sure he'll be delighted to help if he can."

"Now then, how are you keeping?" Tom asked, although he could see the answer.

"I'm OK, except for this bloody arthritis – it keeps me down and I don't like it."

Tom thought how carefully Laura had been moving around the kitchen.

"I don't get out as much as I'd like to. Some days I can't get as far as the car, never mind get in it! But it's not been too bad for the last day or so."

Tom knew how hard it must have been for Laura to get to the cottage to see him, and he felt guilty for not having been there to greet her. The latch on the back door rattled and he heard his boss's voice as he bade goodbye to someone across the yard. As Jack Deacon pulled off his boots and came in, Laura filled another mug from the pot on the Aga. He beamed at the sight of his most trusted employee sitting at the long table. "Well then, Tom, how's the world with you?" he said, and he washed his shovel-like hands under the tap before shaking them dry.

"I'm OK, boss," Tom replied.

"Tom needs to talk to you," Laura said, handing Jack his tea.

"Oh, that sounds ominous," Jack replied.

"Don't mind me," said Laura. "I'll make myself scarce."

"No," said Tom. "What I have to say involves all of us. That is, if you don't mind."

Laura turned and sat down again. "Now it does sound serious," she said.

The Deacons looked at Tom with concerned faces, and then he began. "I don't really know where to start, but, well, I've had a few shocks while getting Dad's affairs in order."

"Is it money, Tom? I'll help if I can," said Jack.

"Well, yes, it is money, but not in the way you might think. It seems that Dad had rather more than I thought."

"Well, that's good, isn't it?" said Jack.

"I don't really know. I'm not used to this sort of thing and it's worrying me."

"OK," said Jack. "Well, we can help you out there. Have you got it in the bank or a building society? Because it should be earning you interest, you know."

"The thing is, it's not just money – it's land as well."

"Land? Well, that's different. Is it around here?"

"Err, yes," Tom confirmed. He shifted around on his seat and avoided eye contact with Jack. He felt like a naughty child.

"How did he come by it?" Jack asked.

"It was left to him by someone."

"Well, well." Jack sat back in his chair.

"The thing is, before I tell you any more, I have to clear something up." Tom shuffled on his chair as he spoke. He could feel Laura's eyes on him, but he could not bear to look. "You two have been good to me – far more than just employers. I count you as my friends, and I don't want that to change."

"You're not making sense, Tom," said Jack. "We're glad that you feel like that, but what's all this about?"

Laura lifted her head. "Emily Margesson," she said softly. "Am I right?"

"Yes," said Tom, looking hard at his hands.

The pendulum of the grandfather clock by the door seemed to hammer against the sides of the case, shattering the silence that made time hang and run in slow motion.

"I don't understand," said Jack, standing up and shaking his head.

"She left Dad money and land, and I don't know what else." Tom had now passed the point of no return. He wondered to himself how Laura knew about Emily.

Jack walked over to the window. "Well, I never," he said. "I knew there was talk a few years back about those two..." He broke off when Laura shot him a stern look.

Tom couldn't hold back any longer. "The fact is, she left Dad nearly everything she had; Larkspur House – and Glebe Farm." His hands were shaking and he could feel the sweat forming around his neck and brow. He just wanted to run out of the door, but at the same time he didn't want to look up from his hands for fear of what he might see in his employers' faces.

"Well, that's a canny fortune, Tom, and no mistake," said Jack. Tom looked up to see Laura smiling at him. "So there was some truth in the talk about those two!" Jack added.

"Shut up!" Laura snapped, leaving her husband in no doubt that he'd been tactless. She turned to Tom. "Are you alright? You didn't know before, did you?"

"No, I didn't have a clue. Now the solicitors tell me there are hundreds of thousands of pounds in the bank, and then there is Larkspur, farmland and shares. What do I know about shares? I still think there's been some error, but have a look at this – this is what the solicitors gave me."

He handed Jack the list of the contents of the box. There was silence for a while as Jack read, while Laura peered over his shoulder.

"Well, you're a rich man now, Tom Dwyer." He turned to Laura. "It looks like we might have a new landlord!" he laughed.

"That's the bit I really hate," said Tom.

"Don't be daft!" said Laura, and she smiled in Tom's direction.

Jack handed the piece of paper back to Tom. "You need professional help with this lot," he said. "This needs a better brain than mine, and besides, I have some interest here; it wouldn't be right for me to advise you."

Feeling hugely relieved, Tom explained about the afternoon's encounter at the solicitor's office. Jack and Laura listened intently, without saying a word. "So, there it is," he concluded. "I am confused and worried about the whole thing."

It was Laura who spoke first. "You've got a good man in Martin Stone – you can trust him to guide you, but watch Dyson, Tom, just watch him. He's a..."

"Now then, Laura, don't start all that." Jack stopped her going any further. "The truth is, Tom, we're in a bit of a battle with Dyson about our rent and Laura's taken against him. But he's just a hard-nosed businessman – we'll sort him out, don't you worry about that."

"Well, if it belongs to me, then I'll sort it out," replied Tom indignantly.

"You can't do that, Tom. You let to Miss Aldridge and she sublets to me. My dispute is with Dyson on her behalf, it's not with you."

Laura couldn't hold back any longer. "I don't know why she trusts him with her affairs, never mind agreeing to marry him!"

"Now, Laura, it's none of our business!" Jack said angrily.

"I didn't like him at all," said Tom. "I didn't know they were a couple, but I did wonder. She just introduced him as her business manager and advisor."

Laura was clearly not going to let go. "Advisor! Well, I'd like to give Miss Aldridge some advice, but it would be about him! He's a liar, Jack, and you know he is. Tell Tom what he's done."

"I'm not going to involve Tom in all of that," Jack insisted.

"I'd rather know," said Tom.

Jack reluctantly began to explain. "The fact is, he came here three or four months ago asking me to pay him the rent in cash. He said the office systems were down and he needed the money a little earlier, as it would take longer to process. I went to the bank and got it – about ten thousand. I was stupid enough not to get a receipt." Jack was clearly embarrassed and looked down at his hands. "Then we got a bill from Margesson Holdings for the current quarter's rent, as well as the last one – they asked for a settlement for the lot. I rang them and they insisted I hadn't paid anything. Then Dyson came back here with a surveyor. He looked at the buildings and said I wasn't looking after them and they would need repairs. Dyson said he would keep the cash I'd given him for those, so that was why we still owed the full amount for both quarters."

"See what I mean?" said Laura. "You just watch him, Tom."

Tom had never seen Jack and Laura like this before. He also knew that Jack looked after the buildings extremely well. "There is something very wrong here," he said. "I am going to speak to Mr Stone and I think you should do the same. Put this on record."

"OK, I will," said Jack, "but I feel very foolish."

They talked while Laura served up chicken casserole with fresh bread. To keep things safe, they discussed what had been happening on the farm. For the first time in a while,

Tom was able to laugh. As he walked home, he began to feel that things were a little better. At least he could talk about what was happening. However, it was obvious that Dyson was very bad news. As he settled down to sleep, Tom made a decision to tackle the rent issue head on.

Chapter Five

The Reckoning

Surrounded by lush meadow and neatly cropped by grazing sheep and the occasional roe deer, Larkspur House stood resplendent. As Tom stepped onto the gravel drive, two does twitched upright and took off for the cover of the surrounding woodland. Variegated ivy grew over grey stone and was neatly trained around mullioned windows. No cars were in the turning circle in front of the house and Tom wondered if anyone was at home. He pulled on the bell, hoping that Anna Aldridge would be in without Dyson.

An older woman wearing an overall opened the door. "Now then, Tom, what brings you here?"

Tom had known Nora Marchant for most of his life and it came back to him that she worked as a housekeeper at Larkspur. "Hello, Nora. I need a word with Miss Aldridge, if possible?"

Nora looked puzzled, but invited Tom in and asked him to take a seat in the hallway. She left him there and did not return for some time. While he was waiting, Tom studied the oak panelled walls and the patterned stone tile floor, which was probably bigger than the entire ground floor of his cottage. Then he spotted a portrait of Anna Aldridge hanging above the large fireplace. It was beautifully painted and the artist had captured her in a classic pose, seated at an oak writing desk with her chin propped on her hand, seemingly deep in thought. Tom stood up to read the inscription on the bottom of the frame, but before he was close enough to see it clearly, he was startled by Anna's voice behind him. "Beautiful, wasn't she?"

Tom turned quickly. "Err, yes, very," he said, realising that the painting couldn't be of Anna.

"She had it painted for her fortieth birthday, before 'the wrinkles set in', as she always said. Ever the realist was my grandmother, but I imagine you did not come here to look at paintings, Mr Dwyer?"

"No, err, no, of course not. I need to follow up on our conversation yesterday."

"Oh, OK, come through to the library. I'll ask Nora to make us some tea."

"Not for me," said Tom, feeling that this may not be an easy encounter. The midmorning sun streamed in through the large bay window. Lining the walls were more books than Tom had ever seen in one place. The sunlight glinted on gold designs embossed on the leather spines of the books, which covered the walls either side of the fireplace in neat, uniform sets. Anna directed Tom towards two easy chairs by a low table in the bay window. Taking a seat, he looked out of the window onto the beautifully laid-out garden. A pair of roe deer quietly licked the sweet tops of the new grass on the lawn, and two robins took their feed from a large bird table.

"I've been thinking about Jack Deacon and what you said about his rent."

"Oh?"

"Yes, if you can let me know how much he's outstanding, I will see to it that it's paid. I would like to help them and I also thought it might help you to have the money."

"It would," Anna replied, "but I don't think it's your responsibility to settle up."

"No, but if you could just tell me how much, I will get Mr Stone to see to it that it's paid at once."

"You really need to speak to Alex about this – he'll be back any time now," said Anna, looking slightly uncomfortable.

"I only need to know how much," Tom reiterated.

"I'll need to check the exact amount with Alex, but we're talking about nearly £20,000."

At that moment, the library door opened and Alex Dyson strode in. "Mr Dwyer," he said, surprised to see Tom there.

Anna looked even more uncomfortable "Err, Mr Dwyer wants to pay the outstanding rent on Glebe Farm," she explained.

By this time, Dyson had opened the cocktail cabinet and was in the midst of pouring himself a drink. As Anna spoke, he temporarily froze. And, with his back to both of them, said, "That's a matter for the Deacons ... it doesn't concern anyone else."

Tom stood up. "Well, I've discussed it fully with Jack and Laura. I know all of the details except the amount outstanding." Yet again, his assertiveness took him by surprise.

As Dyson turned around, Tom fixed on him with a cold stare, causing him to turn away and look out of the window. With his back to Tom, he said, "I'll look it up and let you know in a day or so."

"I'd rather know now," said Tom.

Dyson spun around "And I said I will let you know," he replied, his expression fixed in a glare.

"OK," said Tom. "I want it in writing tomorrow. I also expect it to take into account any cash paid to you on account."

"Oh, there's nothing like that," said Anna.

"Isn't there?" said Tom, looking straight at Dyson. Once again, Dyson turned his back and looked out of the window. He was silent for a moment.

"Alex?" said Anna, assuming that Dyson didn't realise he was expected to give an answer.

"Err, no, nothing on account," he said, without turning around.

"That's funny," said Tom. "Jack and Laura told me they'd given you a substantial amount of cash."

"Alex?" Anna was clearly puzzled.

"Oh, rubbish!" he said. "They're just embarrassed because they can't pay and they don't want to admit it to one of their 'employees'".

Anna looked at Tom. "We will let you know the exact amount," she said, before walking towards the door.

Tom followed. "Before I go, just one more thing," he said. "I'm concerned that your surveyor wasn't happy with the state of the property. I'll speak with Mr Stone and I'll probably need to get my own inspection done, especially as there's some concern that it's not in good shape."

"What surveyor?" Anna said sharply.

"The one who told the Deacons they're not maintaining the buildings properly."

"It was someone from Michael Wright Surveyors," Dyson told Anna. "I just wanted to turn the heat up a bit. That place is worth more than we are getting for it. The Deacons need to retire if they can't afford it."

"Well," said Tom, "they're worried sick. I'll speak to Mr Stone about a survey of the whole estate – it seems like a good idea. I'll be on my way now. I'll expect to hear from you tomorrow."

As Anna showed Tom to the door, he felt very uneasy about leaving. He knew he'd provoked some questions between Anna and Dyson that would undoubtedly result in a row. As he walked back across the turning circle, he stopped to look at Dyson's low-slung sports car and noted that it was a Lamborghini. It was classy, but it seemed cramped. He was about to turn down the gravel drive when Nora Marchant came from the side of the house, pushing a bicycle. "Well," she said. "I don't know what you said to those two, but you've put the cat amongst the pigeons and that's a fact. As soon as the door closed behind you, he was shouting the place down. I'm glad to be out of there."

"Really?" said Tom. "I thought as much. What do you know about him, Nora?"

"Not very much, but that's more than I'd like to know!"

"Why's that?"

"I hate being there when he's in – the whole place has an awful atmosphere. He's like a bear with a sore head most of the time and I think he's a bully. He often reduces Miss Aldridge to tears."

"Does he live there, Nora?"

"Some of the time, but he has business in London, which often takes him away Thursday until Tuesday. Miss

Aldridge is a different person for that time. What brings you up here anyway? Moving in these circles doesn't seem like your bag."

"Just a bit of business," said Tom.

"Well," said Nora, "if you've shaken hands with him I should be sure to count your fingers!"

With that, she got on her bicycle and pushed away.

As he walked down the lane, Tom turned over in his head all that he knew and suspected about Dyson and Anna Aldridge. Lost in his thoughts, he didn't hear the approach of the vehicle that struck him and threw him sideways into a bramble ditch.

A searing pain shot through his right shoulder and his head struck something hard. A feeling of cold washed through his body and, as he drifted towards darkness, his thoughts tumbled over and over. He became aware of a face looking down at him, speaking words he couldn't hear. Then the darkness closed over him and, after some time, somewhere in the distance, he heard another voice calling to him, as he spiralled through a long tunnel.

The darkness began to dissolve. The pain in his head was distracting, but he managed a squint and saw a man's shape. "Try and stay with me. What's your name?"

Tom tried to answer, but somehow he couldn't make it happen. It slowly came to his attention that he was now in a very small room with dark windows. He tried to sit up.

"It's OK, it's OK. You're in an ambulance, you've had a fall."

Tom remembered falling. "Oh, my head!" he said. His mouth was bone dry and he couldn't form his words properly. "I need a drink."

"Not just yet, we're going to get you to hospital, then we'll see."

The man was now shining a torch in Tom's eyes. "He's conscious," he said over his shoulder. "Any time now would be good."

The ambulance started up and Tom felt it pull away. In a short time, the siren started wailing in short bursts. Once again, he tried to sit up, but the sharp pain in his shoulder stopped him.

"Now, you must be still," said the man, as he took Tom's pulse. "Just for a few more minutes. Do you remember what happened?"

"Not really. One minute I was walking and the next I was down."

"OK, OK, well, all of that can be sorted out later. Let's just get you to hospital."

The ambulance eventually came to a halt and the back doors opened. Over the following hour, Tom was examined and X-rayed from every angle, before being left to rest on a trolley in a cubicle. He was asked several times what had happened to him, but he honestly didn't know. All he could remember was the first face looking down at him ... a face he could easily name but had decided not to. Until he understood more, he would say nothing about it.

He was dozing on the trolley when someone drew the curtains of the cubicle and came in. It was a young police officer from Downfield Station. He introduced himself as PC Jarvis. "We're trying to establish what happened to you, Mr Dwyer. I need to ask you some questions. Before your fall, do you remember seeing or hearing anyone else in the lane?"

"No," Tom replied. "The last thing I can remember is speaking to Nora Marchant before she got on her bike and rode away. A few minutes later ... well, I just don't know."

"You mentioned Nora Marchant – who's that?" PC Jarvis was making notes.

"She lives next door to the post office, which is very close to where I live. She's Miss Aldridge's housekeeper."

"OK, well, we'll have a word with her. There's not much to go on at the moment, I'm afraid. Are you sure you can't remember anything?"

"No, nothing. How did they find me?" Tom asked.

"Ah, someone called 999 and reported that you were lying in a ditch. The ambulance was with you in a few minutes. Unfortunately, the person who called didn't leave their name. The doctor thinks you were hit by a car. Do you remember hearing one?

"I don't think so," said Tom.

Eventually, a doctor came in and told Tom that he'd sustained no serious injuries, just a badly bruised shoulder and mild concussion, along with cuts from the brambles.

"You were very lucky – it could have been an awful lot worse. I'm afraid you're going to be pretty uncomfortable for a day or so. We'll give you some painkillers and I would like you to rest up for a while."

After some strong arguments, the doctor agreed to let Tom go home, but only on the condition that he allowed him to call the Deacons so he wouldn't be leaving the hospital alone.

Jack arrived in quick time. Tom apologised for dragging him out and explained, as best he could, what had happened.

"Have you told Martin Stone?"

"Uh, no," said Tom.

"You should – there's just about time to catch him now before he leaves the office." Jack dialled the number on the payphone and gave Stone a brief outline of the day's events. He also mentioned that Tom had been talking with Dyson. He turned to Tom as he rang off. "Now, I'm instructed to take you back to the farm, Tom. You can argue about it with Laura. Martin Stone's going to call by in an hour or so."

Laura was standing in the yard as they drove in, clearly keen to see for herself how Tom was and ready, as ever, to know how she could help. She opened the passenger door and Tom tried to get out of the old Mercedes. Turning and pulling were both agony, but he managed to get out and make his way into the kitchen.

Once settled, he began to go through the story once again for Jack and Laura. At this point, Martin Stone arrived, which meant Tom had to backtrack and start the story all over again. "Well, there it is," he said. Not much of a tale, is it? We'll probably never know exactly what happened. I think someone in a hurry just came too close – if they'd been just a bit further over, I would probably be pushing up the daisies!"

"Do you think Dyson had something to do with it?" asked Laura.

"I don't think so," Tom said.

He now remembered quite clearly the face that had looked down on him in the ditch, but he was steadfast in his resolve not to say anything.

"Well, you should tell the police about your conversation with him," Laura said emphatically.

"No," said Tom. "I want to let things rest. I need to get back to the cottage."

"Oh no you don't!" Laura said. "Not tonight. The spare room is made up ready for you. We'll see how you are in the morning."

Tom was so tired that he gave in. He managed to walk with Stone out to the yard. "Err, there's two things," he said. "Whatever we're offered, the shares for Margesson Holdings are not for sale. Second, please find out all you can about the company for me. What do they hold? I have no proof, but I know that Dyson is up to no good."

"Be careful, Tom," said Stone. "Work through me if you can, and don't take risks. I told you before, he's tricky, and maybe worse."

"Indeed," said Tom. "Indeed."

Chapter Six

A Secret Love

The following morning, Tom was awake early, but it took him longer than usual to get washed and dressed. It seemed that every bone and muscle in his body was screaming at him. Just getting downstairs took all of the effort he could muster. Laura was sitting at the table in the kitchen, and the clock by the door was striking seven. "Come and sit yourself down. How are you feeling?" she asked.

"Huh, like I've been threshed and bailed," Tom replied. The sight before him was a welcome delight. Laura's breakfasts were part of Tom's daily working life and he'd really missed them. The plate before him had on it bacon, egg and sausage, along with toast with lashings of butter. With two of the painkillers from the hospital, Laura's fry up and several cups of tea inside him, Tom was already feeling stronger. "I need to be getting off," he said. "Thank you for letting me stay and for everything that you've done."

"I knew you'd be anxious to go," Laura replied, "but remember that you can stay as long as you like."

"No," said Tom. "I need to get back."

"Then I'll take you."

"No, no you don't. It's harder for you than it is for me!"

"Rubbish!" Laura exclaimed.

At that point, Jack came in from the yard. "Hello! Now, what are you two arguing about on this lovely morning?"

"Tom doesn't want me to take him home. He's just being stubborn."

Jack laughed. "Now, there's the pot calling the kettle if ever I heard it!" he said. "Well, I'm taking Tom and that's final, so stop it both of you. In a day or two, when you're up to it, you can take the pickup, Tom. I won't need it now until the end of next week, and even then I can manage without it. Now that you've got a little bit of money, you should see about getting yourself some wheels, it would help you to get about more. Let me know if you need some help with finding something suitable."

"Thanks, boss," said Tom, "it will be a real help to borrow the pickup, thank you, but I don't think I'm fit to drive it yet."

On their way back to the cottage, they stopped at the shop to buy some groceries. Tom was so glad to get home. Once alone, he looked at himself in the kitchen mirror. *Oh, heck,* he said to himself. *What a mess!* His face had been badly scratched by the brambles and there was a substantial bruise over his left temple and eye. He looked even worse than he felt. Without his razor at Jack and Laura's, he hadn't been able to shave and his stubbly shadow didn't help matters. Getting rid of his fuzz was painful because of the scratches, but he felt better for it. Afterwards, he managed to drag the easy chair from the kitchen into the garden, and he flopped into it with the last bit of effort he had in him. With the sun on his face, he soon drifted off to sleep. As he opened his eyes, he saw Alex Dyson walking up the garden path.

"My, my," he said. "Nora said you'd taken a bit of a knock, but I didn't expect anything quite like this. You look done in, old chap. Have they got any leads on what hit you?"

"I'm not sure," said Tom. "Did you want something?"

"Uh, yes. I just wanted a word about the Deacons."

"Well?"

"I've come to let you know that Anna and I have decided not to deal with you on this matter. It really is between us and the tenant."

"Oh, have you now? Anna and I, is it?" Tom got up from the chair, ignoring his pain. He could feel his anger welling up inside. "Well, now let me tell you something. You might think you're clever, and that you're dealing with a fool, but just remember this: while you're being the snake in the grass, this fool owns the field, and he intends to smoke you out."

"I do hope that's not a threat, Mr Dwyer," Dyson smirked. "Well, in that case I'll just get off and leave you to it. I'll tell Anna you're still alive – she was foolish enough to be concerned. It's a female thing."

"Well, you just tell her I'm fine."

"Look, Mr Dwyer, please believe that neither of us mean you any harm. We've put in an offer for your shares of Margesson Holdings. I'm sure Mr Stone will be advising you to accept it."

"Oh, really?" said Tom, "well, we'll see about that."

Dyson swaggered away down the garden path. For the first time ever, Tom wished he had a telephone to speak to

Stone. He spent the rest of the day sorting through papers from the sitting room. He placed some of them in black sacks for the rubbish and the rest in cardboard boxes.

The drawers of the writing desk hadn't been cleared for decades. Tom pulled each one out and shook the dust that had built up inside them onto the floor. When he went to push the bottom one back in, he found it would only go about half way. *"Bugger!"* he said out loud. *"What's wrong with it?"*

With difficulty, he got down on his hands and knees to see what the problem was. He couldn't see anything, so he pushed his arm inside. At once, the obstruction was obvious – it seemed like a book had fallen flat inside. He pulled it out to discover it wasn't a book at all, but a King Edward cigar box. Replacing the drawer, he sat down and opened the box. It contained some photographs, a few papers and a green, leather ring box. As he removed the items, a photo of a woman looked up at him. It was the same face that was in the painting at Larkspur House. By the age of the photograph, Tom knew it must be Emily Margesson, but in every other way it could have been Anna. On the back, a faded, careful hand had written, *"Ka'Lani"*. Beneath that were the words, *"To J, with all of my love, forever. I wish so much that you were here. No matter what, this will always be our place. E."*

Tom looked at the photograph again. Emily was seated in a wicker chair by a table, on a veranda overlooking the ocean. She had a pen in her hand and appeared poised to write. In the top right-hand corner of the picture, a palm tree drooped its long fronds.

Where on earth can that be? Tom thought. He set the picture aside. The ring box contained a gold ring with a large emerald. Tom checked the picture again and focused on the hand holding the pen. Emily's ring looked the same. The box also contained a collection of other photos; a young couple lounging by a pool in modest swimsuits; the same pair holding hands as they walked along the beach, and a rather dapper young man raising a glass at a picnic. The young John Dwyer cut an impressive figure. He was tall with broad shoulders and an open face. His smile spoke of contentment and genuine honesty. The likeness of father and son was easy to see, but Tom couldn't remember his father ever looking so happy.

More letters from Emily were tied together in a bundle, some of them relatively recent. One had been kept in its envelope and was addressed to Mr J Dwyer, c/o Stone, Blackman & Co. It was marked: *"To be held at the office, for collection."* Tom opened it – this time, the letter was typed.

"My Dearest J,

I did not get to read your last letter until now and I am sorry to hear that you are not well. I wish with all of my heart that I could be near you, but I am unable to go anywhere now. Here sits the body of a feeble old woman, who can no longer tie her own shoelaces, do up her own buttons or brush her own hair. But believe me when I say that my mind and heart remain as young as ever.

J, I still feel the fire of our love burning deep within me, and the happy memories of our past are still vivid in a profusion of colour. Life has been so cruel to us, J, but I would not change a thing. The time we spent together was so perfect and I know that it held more love than some people experience in their entire lives. The memories of our last time together burn bright and will be with me always.

Dr Mills came today, and although he smiles and tells me that things are going along fine, I know that my time is short. I do wish he wouldn't patronise me like a child!

Before I begin to lose my mind (I'm sure they think I already have!), I need to entrust you with a task, J. My dear Anna is without doubt all I could have wished for in a granddaughter - she's clever, artistic, caring and sensitive, and when you consider all that she's been through, it's amazing that she's the well-balanced person she is.

However, there is a vulnerability in her, which, when coupled with her stubbornness (I cannot imagine where she gets that from!), is a big worry. She's formed a friendship with a man called Alex Dyson, whom she loves and intends to marry. I do not trust this man. I have discussed this with Bernard Lyle of Baverstock and Lyle, and he shares my opinion. I have therefore provided for Anna in leaving her half my shares in Margesson Holdings (not a controlling interest) and a small trust, which will run until she is forty-five. She will then be given a modest lump sum, and that's it. I really feel, J, that if I give her more, he will bleed her dry. If he does, I leave you the key to our box in Lahaina. I've kept it up for as long as I can.

I ask that you do all you can to ensure she does not have to leave the house unless it's absolutely necessary.

The HANA Trust is still as we set it up and is now in your name. It seems that it's quite healthy and therefore should provide for Anna well if it needs to. As for the rest of my belongings, and my estate, I've left them to you. I feel it's the least I can do - had we been together, as we should have been, then it would have been yours by rights anyway. I also leave you the other half of my share of Margesson Holdings. While you have a hand in it, I know that right will be done and that you will be a stabilising influence. It was, after all, your advice and guidance that made the most of the money in the first place. So, please, J, take it, spend it and give yourself and Thomas the life you should have had - and don't let that stupid pride of yours stand in the way.

I hope you are feeling better soon, and I will try and write again, but whatever happens, I give you all of my love, always.

Em

Tom contemplated what he had just read. So, even more responsibility was tied up with this money than he'd initially thought. Could that be another reason why Dad didn't want to spend it? He closed the letter and placed it on the pile with the others.

Emily's heartfelt words had cleared up so many things for Tom. He was now clear that she and his father loved each other deeply. All his suspicions about Dyson had been confirmed, too. Emily had clearly sussed him out before she died, and Tom thought how her fears were coming true.

Chapter Seven

A Face from the Darkness

Tom decided to discuss the letters he had found with Stone as soon as possible. He continued to clear the writing desk, which contained no more surprises other than a copy of the papers concerning his mother's divorce of his father on the grounds of adultery. They named Emily Margesson as a correspondent. This had never been discussed with Tom, but from conversations he'd overheard in the house as a youngster, he'd suspected there could have been someone else involved. He knew so little about his father. In fact, over recent weeks, he had realised that he'd hardly known him at all. He'd been a remote figure in his and Ella's lives when they were children, and he only engaged, played or read to them on special days and holidays. Later on, after Mother left, he became rather stern and short tempered, only occasionally letting down his guard and showing the warmer, kind person that he kept deep inside. When he became ill, Tom cared for him without question. For the most part, his father was demanding and at times extremely unkind. Looking back, Tom thought how there were a few occasions towards the end when Dad could have been on the verge of opening up, but he couldn't quite bring himself to do it. These memories suddenly made Tom fill up with anger. *What a bloody mess he's left me to clear up – and all because he wanted to keep his head stuck in the sand. Why didn't he spend some of this money?*

Of course, Tom knew the answer. If his father had used the money he would have had to explain where it came from. And he could never have done that – he was far too proud and stubborn.

The next piece of the puzzle was not long in coming.

To Tom's relief, the next day did not involve meetings with lawyers and he resolved to carry on with clearing the sitting room; it felt therapeutic somehow, and yesterday's revelation about Dad and Emily Margesson had made him realise how his father's life had held great sadness as well as great love. He wanted to know more.

As he was filling the final rubbish sack, the sound of the front door knocker made him jump. Tom decided it was the Deacons checking up on him, so he was very surprised to see Anna Aldridge on the doorstep.

"Good morning, Mr Dwyer, I was just wondering how you are. I hope you are recovering well?"

Tom noticed how pale she looked. Her eyes were red and she seemed anxious, too. He led her around to the back door and into the rather untidy kitchen. Once inside, he quickly removed a full rubbish sack from the only armchair. "I'm fine," he said. "There's nothing broken, I'm just a bit sore."

"I wanted to tell you first, but I am about to go to the police station to confess. I am afraid it was me who ran you down. I am so terribly sorry and I need to set the record straight. Please believe that it was an accident. Alex and I had a terrible row and I drove off. I was crying so much that

I just did not see you."

"I know," said Tom calmly.

"You know?"

"Yes, I remember you looking down at me when I was in the ditch. It was you who called the ambulance, wasn't it?"

"Yes, but ... have you already told the police, then?"

"No, and I am not going to," Tom said firmly, "and neither are you."

"But I must put things straight. I've been very stupid and I need to face up to things."

"No, you will just get into trouble. You have said you didn't mean it and I believe you, so no harm done."

"My grandmother would be ashamed of me," Anna said.

"I doubt it."

"Did you know her?"

"No, but I am beginning to," Tom said. "Now, no more talk of going to the police. I will ask Mr Stone to get them to stop the investigation, so that should make everything right."

"Thank you, Mr Dwyer, that is more kindness than I deserve. I stopped to see that you were OK and I called the police from the phone box on the corner. I stayed until I heard the ambulance and then I went back to Larkspur. I was frightened, you see. I am so glad you're all right, but I am sure I should tell the police. Alex said not to as it will mean a definite ban from driving, but I don't care – it's the right thing."

"Ban? Not for a genuine accident, surely?" said Tom.

"Well, probably not under normal circumstances, but I have taken the blame for some speeding offences of Alex's, so my record does not look good. But that's not your problem and I really should do the right thing. My grandmother would not rest easy if she felt I had done anything like this without owning up. She still haunts everything I do. I am so very sorry, Mr Dwyer. If there is anything I can do, please just say."

Tom paused thoughtfully for a few seconds before replying, "Well, there are a few things as a matter of fact."

Anna looked surprised. "OK," she said, "ask away and I will do them if I can."

Tom looked her straight in the face. "Well, first of all, I want you to put any thought of going to the police right out of your head."

"Why?" She looked puzzled.

"Because I believe it was an accident and there is no reason for you to lose your licence just because you've helped Mr Dyson. However, I do think that was a stupid and wrong thing to do."

"I know, but..." She tailed off.

"I will tell them that I have got over the bang on the head and, having remembered everything, I'm quite sure I fell. The other thing is that I would like to know more about your grandmother. It's really so that I can learn more about my father and their relationship. You see, I know very little and so much of this has been a surprise to me."

Anna smiled as she thought of Emily Margesson. "She was a wonderful woman and never made a bad judgement in her life, except possibly for agreeing to marry Victor. If she loved and trusted your father, and it seems like she probably did, then he must have been a very special person."

"That's just it," said Tom. "I don't know that he was. I've only just realised now that I never really knew him."

Tom went to the sitting room, took out the photo from the box and handed it to Anna. She examined it before reading the note on the back. "Wow, what a love story!"

"Do you know where it is?"

"Oh yes, without a doubt it was taken at Makena, on the island of Maui."

"Where's that?" Tom had no clue.

"It's one of the Hawaiian Islands, in the Pacific. Grandmother owned a property there – Ka'Lani. We had an interest in producing coffee in Hawaii for a while and when that was done she couldn't bring herself to sell the place. She loved it so much. I'm sure you must own it now."

"I don't think so, but I will ask Mr Stone to find out. There are also many letters from your grandmother, but those are with the solicitors."

"I have some from your father, too," Anna replied. "Would you like to see them?"

Tom couldn't resist the chance to know more. "Yes, I think I would."

Anna stood up. "Look, I really should go now. Alex will be wondering where I am and he would be furious if he knew. How about tomorrow? I would love to see my grandmother's letters. Could you get them?"

"Well, yes, I suppose so," said Tom.

"So, let's say three? You could come to Larkspur for afternoon tea?"

"Yes, that's fine. I don't want to get into another battle with Mr Dyson, though."

"You won't. He's in the US from tomorrow morning until next week."

"In that case, I will be there," Tom replied with a smile.

Anna looked him straight in the face. "I really do appreciate your understanding, Mr Dwyer. I am so very sorry for the pain I have caused you. May I collect you tomorrow?"

"No, I'm fine. Don't worry, I will get to Larkspur no problem."

Chapter Eight
A Tangled Web

Tom was now clear in his mind that Anna was genuine and that Dyson was, without a doubt, not to be trusted. For some reason, though, Anna had put her faith in him. Emily Margesson had weighed him up correctly and not only did Tom now feel a responsibility to look out for Anna, as Emily had asked his father to do, but he felt a strong desire to ensure that Dyson was brought down a peg or two and exposed for what he was.

As he lay in bed that night, for the first time, Tom began to think about what he might like for himself. He wanted to feel more confident over what he was dealing with and resolved that some new clothes would be a good start – he seldom updated his wardrobe.

First thing the next morning, he took Jack up on his offer to lend him the pickup and went into Downfield. First of all he had a haircut and then he went to a gent's outfitters called Harrowby and Son. Tom knew his father shopped there a long time ago, and before he knew it, he had two new pairs of trousers, a new blazer, three shirts and a pair of shoes. It was a great surprise to Tom that they had things that fit him. His extremely broad shoulders were usually a problem when it came to jackets. Back at home, he checked himself out in the mirror. As he pulled his shoulders back and extended himself to his full five feet ten inches, he admitted to himself that the new haircut made the best of his receding hairline and that the white shirt showed off his tanned skin, earned from working outside throughout the summer. He cut what he decided was an average figure, but even with his glasses on, he felt more confident. He'd made no big style changes, but at least now he would feel a little less out of place in the meetings he was attending.

So much had happened in such a short space of time, and most of it was a million miles from Tom's regular life. His meetings with Anna were revealing and beginning to answer some of his questions. He sensed that Anna was embarrassed and uncomfortable over the way her fiancée was behaving. It was as though Dyson was controlling her. Tom could also see that Anna was trying to piece together her grandmother's story in much the same way as he was trying to identify his father's. It was obvious from the letters that his father and Emily Margesson had been very much in love. It was clear that they found in each other something that could not be found in anyone else. Tom thought how hard it must have been to live with all of that secrecy. It was obvious how much they wanted to be together, but also how impossible that was too.

He remembered that when he was very small, his father was forced to leave his job as manager on the Margesson estate. Tom had never understood why, he just knew they had moved to the small cottage that was now home in a hurry. This was the reason why so much of their furniture was far too big. He recalled how their first house had been much bigger and really quite grand. He thought of how upset his mother had been when they moved, and it was true that she had never forgiven John Dwyer for their loss of status. Tom hadn't known the reason for his father having to leave his job, but now it seemed that his relationship with Emily probably had something to do with it. He needed to find out more.

Laura Deacon was as pleased as ever to see Tom and was pouring the tea out while he was barely in the door. Tom asked her outright if she would tell him what she knew about his father and Emily Margesson.

"Oh, no! You don't want to go raking all that up. It was nothing."

Tom explained about the letters. "You see, I really don't think it was nothing," he said.

"Well, it will do you no good to meddle in those things – they are all in the past."

But Laura could see that Tom was unconvinced and, after all, he probably had a right to know. "Well, if you must know, yes, they did have an affair it seems. No one really knew until the incident and then it all came out and spread round the village like wildfire."

"So, what happened?"

"Well, to start with, Victor Margesson was a nasty piece of work. He was a handsome devil and he knew it. He had women all over the county and lived a lord's lifestyle without ever having a penny to call his own – his own family cut him off after some trouble at home.

"As a young man, he was sent away to Ceylon, where I think his family had business, but the money and the entrepreneurial spirit belonged to Emily. Her father was a diplomat, as was his father before him. They were also in business overseas, but the family always lived at Larkspur. Victor was a charmer and he lived in Downfield on what seemed like modest means. I remember other girls being quite envious when he got engaged to Emily.

"Soon after they were married, Victor started getting up to his old tricks of partying and womanising. He lived half his life drunk and the other either recovering or drinking himself into the next round of trouble. He led Emily a merry dance and the rumour was that he was handy with his fists too. Your father comes into the picture because he was the Margesson's estate manager."

"Yes, I knew that, and I knew it all came to a sudden end – we had to move in a hurry."

"Yes, well the story is that Victor and Emily were having an argument at Larkspur and he lashed out at her just as your father was coming into the room. There was a nasty fight and Victor ended up with a broken nose – John was sacked on the spot.

"Well, of course, all that led to questions and before you could turn around the village was alive with rumours about an affair between John and Emily that had apparently gone on for years. In fact, it's been said they were close friends even before either of them were married. But I am not sure how true that is."

"That would explain some of the early photos I've seen," said Tom.

"Only a year or so after that, Victor Margesson came to grief in a hunting accident – he was killed instantly in a fall. To be honest, there weren't many tears shed in the village, as by then he'd revealed his true character and was considered a deeply unpleasant man."

"What about my mother, did she know?"

"Oh yes. I think she knew long before anyone else, but her main concern was you and Ella."

Tom nodded. "I knew they weren't happy, but as a child you don't really ask why."

He suddenly felt sad for both his parents; neither of them lived the life they really wanted. He remembered when his mother finally left – he had felt that it was his fault and he couldn't understand what he had done wrong.

He thanked Laura for her honesty. "Just one more thing," he said. "Why didn't Dad and Emily see each other after my mother left and Victor died?"

"I think they were trapped in the lives they had built without each other, and they didn't want their families dragged through any more gossip. Times were different then, Tom." Then she added, quoting a Walter Scott poem, "Oh! What a tangled web we weave, when first we practice to deceive."

After lunch, Tom made his way to Larkspur, as arranged. The heat from the autumn sun was cooling and a chilly breeze was just beginning to shake early leaves from the trees. The old house still looked splendid beneath a greyer sky, as the covering of ivy had started to change colour ready for the next season of the year.

Before Tom parked, Anna Aldridge had opened the front door and invited him in. She showed him straight to the library. "Would you like tea or coffee?" she asked. After Tom had asked for a coffee, she added, "You make yourself comfortable there and I will go and do it. Nora isn't in today."

Tom felt more at peace here than he had the last time, but even though he knew Dyson was meant to be away, he was still dreading his appearance. A pile of letters had been placed on the coffee table between the two chairs and Tom took from his pocket the ones he had retrieved from Stone, along with some from the drawer. He made sure to leave the most incriminating one tucked inside his jacket.

Anna returned with a pot of coffee and some homemade fruitcake. As they sat in the glow of the fire that was burning in the very grand hearth, Tom repeated the story that Laura had told him, carefully missing out some of the more lurid details about Anna's grandfather.

"Well, well," said Anna, when Tom had finished. "So now we know, but to be honest, there are no real surprises there. I never knew Victor, of course, but I have always known that Grandfather was a pretty bad lot. It was my grandmother's sheer determination that saw her through. There's no doubt that she had a sharp business brain."

They sat in silence looking through the letters. After he had read three of them, Tom looked up to see Anna sobbing. "Are you OK?" he asked.

"Yes, I am. Sorry, but I am trying to deal with another serious problem as well as all of this, and it just boiled over."

"Oh, dear. Is there anything I can do?"

Anna regained her composure and shook her head. "No, but you'd better hear about it from me rather than anyone else." She took a deep breath and produced a letter from beside her chair. "I received this yesterday," she said, handing Tom the piece of paper bearing the now familiar Stone, Blackman & Co letterhead. It concerned the rent on Glebe Farm. Clearly, Jack and Laura had taken Tom's advice and asserted that they had paid Dyson in cash.

"You were right, Mr Dwyer," Anna said. "I know the Deacons and they'd never have done this if they weren't sure. So I called Helen Hobbs, the company accountant from Margesson Holdings. She checked and no rent is recorded as having been received from the Deacons. At first it seemed that Alex was right, but then Helen shared with me some of her own concerns. To put it bluntly, I have been a complete fool. Alex is taking substantial amounts of company money, some of it quite illegally, and he's been laundering it through our joint account. I didn't have a clue."

"Oh well," said Tom. "I knew very well that Jack and Laura wouldn't lie like that. I'm so sorry."

"I can't blame anyone but myself," Anna said.

"I'm not sure you can be blamed for what someone else has done."

"The clues have been there, Mr Dwyer, I've just denied them and allowed myself to pretend it was all OK. Just before she died, my grandmother told me that she did not trust Alex, and she warned me that I would regret my loyalty to him. We never disagreed, but we did then. A week or so later, she apologised for interfering and said that she of all people had no business making judgements and remarks like that. She said she would have been much happier if she'd listened to her heart rather than her head and other people's crowing.

"Grandmother never spoke of it again other than to remind me from time to time by saying, 'You must never deny your heart, Anna, it will tell you when you are right and also when you are wrong. But when it does, just make sure you are listening.'"

"Look, I'm sure this can all be put right." Tom said, trying to reassure the still sobbing Anna.

"I doubt it. I will have to find money to replace what has been taken or there will be big trouble. I don't suppose Alex still has it and it may be more than I can find without selling everything I own, such as my shares. But still, that's not your problem."

"Of course it is! If he has stolen from the company then he has stolen from me. I'm a shareholder and if there is a crisis within the company then it is as much my responsibility to put right as it is yours."

Anna had regained her composure and appeared more determined. "Yes, but I will find a way to make sure you and the other shareholders don't lose out."

"Don't you think you have covered up for him enough?"

"Probably," Anna admitted, before giving a sigh and sinking back into the armchair.

"Do you know how much you will have to pay back?" Tom asked.

"Helen is going to do a full audit and let me know, but she thinks it's in the region of £500,000."

"Hell!" said Tom. "What has he done with all that? I suppose that car..."

"The car isn't included, as it's leased by the company. I will need to get it back, and that's easier said than done."

"Well, where is it now? If he's in the States..."

Anna nodded. "Helen thinks that she can get it tracked – it's fitted with a GPS."

"Let's hope that works – at least that will be something."

"I can't do any more until Monday. Helen will stop access to any company money, but I feel bad about it. What if he really was just trying to help me?"

"Well, only you can decide if that was his intention and you can't do that until you know how much and what he's done with it."

Tom thought of the contents of the last letter from Emily and realised that her prophecy was coming true, and with incredible timing. He knew what he had to do, but not yet. "Have you considered telling the police?" he asked.

"No! Whatever he has done, we were together through some very good times. I need to speak to him first, but whatever happens, I think it's over between us. Maybe I should sell my shares and make a new start somewhere else."

"That would mean no Margessons would be left on the board."

"I know. My grandmother would be ashamed of me. I have been such an idiot and wasted all of her hard work. No wonder she didn't leave me anything else."

"I don't think she would see it like that," said Tom. "Look, I found a few more letters that were in Dad's desk. Just read some of the later ones – she mentioned you a lot."

Tom handed Anna a pack of letters, not including Emily's last one. In turn, Anna pushed a small mahogany box across the table towards Tom. "You should look at these," she said.

As they read, Tom glanced up to see Anna staring out through the French doors with tear-filled eyes. "You OK?" he asked.

"Oh, yes," she said peacefully. "I am fine. Some of these letters are just so beautiful. They were so much in love."

"No doubt about that," said Tom.

"I do miss her so," said Anna.

Tom reached into his pocket. "I have something else here that I think you should have." He handed Anna the green leather ring box.

Anna opened it and gave a shallow gasp. "I have wondered so many times where this was. She was wearing it in the painting in the hall."

"I'd like you to have it," said Tom.

"I couldn't," Anna replied, handing it back.

"No, I insist. I have no use for it and I feel sure she would want you to have it."

Tom thought of Emily's wishes in her last letter.

"Do you know what this must be worth?" Anna asked.

"I have no idea," said Tom, "and I don't care. But I believe that I know what it is worth to you, and now it's back in its rightful place, which makes me feel better."

"I don't know what to say. You're a good man, Mr Dwyer. This ring means more to me than you can possibly know."

"That's good. Now, do you think it might be worth a cup of tea?"

"Oh, I am so sorry. I've been so wrapped up in myself. I will get some on the go and then I want to read some more."

Tom followed Anna out into the hall, pausing to look again at the painting of Emily Margesson. She seemed to be staring right into his eyes. Tom shivered, before smiling and following Anna through to the kitchen, which was enormous by Tom's standards. A kettle already hissed on the Aga and then the telephone rang, adding to the din. Anna picked up the kitchen extension. "Larkspur House? Oh, hello, Helen. Where? Oh, my! Yes, Mr Dwyer is here with me now. Hold on, I will ask him."

Anna held the phone close to her shoulder. "Are you up for an urgent board meeting on Tuesday?"

"Well, err, yes," said Tom.

Anna continued her conversation with Helen for a few minutes before ringing off. She said nothing for a while, as she placed two mugs on the table and fetched milk from the fridge. Then she said: "They found the car – it's parked just a few miles away, on the other side of Oxford. I was expecting it to be at Heathrow. Helen is getting her husband to go with her to fetch it tomorrow – we have a spare key."

The hurt Anna was feeling inside was visible on her face as she poured the tea. "I need food!" she said. "How about you?"

"Well, I would be lying if I said I couldn't eat something," said Tom.

They ate fresh bread, cheese and salad, followed by one of Nora Marchant's scones. Tom explained how apprehensive he was about the meeting in London on Monday with Baverstock and Lyle, and now there was a board meeting on Tuesday. "Until this week, I don't think I've ever sat in such serious meetings," he laughed.

"You had better get used to it – it's the way things are done when you have money," said Anna.

"I suppose so, but I don't understand it. I don't know who to go to for advice most of the time."

"Well, you seem to be doing pretty well so far. I'm sure Mr Stone will help," said Anna.

"Yes, he will," Tom replied, but he sounded like he was trying to reassure himself.

"I'd be happy to help you with the board meeting, though there is no reason in the world why you should trust me.

What a mess I've made so far, but I'd be willing to explain what I can."

"I'd be really glad of your help – and I trust you completely."

"But you don't know me," Anna said firmly.

"No, I don't, and it's unusual for me to be so sure about someone so soon, but I am not often wrong about people. I did not like or trust Alex from day one, but I felt sure that you were OK. Besides, I think you and I are on the same journey. We're both trying to piece together our family's dealings and what they have left us with."

Anna smiled and remained silent and in thought as she led the way back into the library. Then she curled up in a large club chair and Tom sat at the desk. The story that was unfolding via the letters was so moving. Occasionally, they would pause and fill each other in on the details. They were both struck by the love between their relatives, and so far they were only about halfway through.

Neither of them paid much attention when the hall clock struck nine. Eventually, Anna put down the letter she was reading, got up from the chair and crossed the room to put more logs on the fire. She drew the curtains across the French windows. "It's turned chilly," she commented.

"I should be going," said Tom. "We can finish this another day."

"We can, but don't rush off on my account. I'm a night owl." Anna picked up more letters and was ready to read on.

"I'm not sure I can focus anymore," said Tom, rubbing his eyes.

"Well, shall I get us some coffee?" Anna was clearly not ready to stop just yet.

"Yes, please, but after that I'll make tracks."

Tom had come to feel even more that Anna was honest, and he wanted to help and protect her. He hadn't felt that way about anyone for a long time. Anna returned with mugs of coffee and a plate of chocolate biscuits. Tom put the letter he was reading back in the box, marking his place with a slip of paper. He sat quietly looking into the fire and sipping his coffee.

"You okay?" Anna's voice was soft and gentle.

Tom thought of Emily's last letter. He knew it would give Anna some assurance, but he decided that now was not the right time to show it to her. "I'm fine," he said, "there's just so much here I didn't know. I can hear my father speaking these words, but it does not seem like the person I knew. I didn't even know he'd been out of the country."

"Well, he had, and a lot more than once. It seems they were going to Ka'Lani before either of them were married. John was there helping my grandfather with estate work, but he was clearly supporting Emily through some difficult times. I think he was her rock."

Anna continued. "It's clear that Ka'Lani was their place," she said, her ensuing sigh reflecting how romantic she found the whole thing.

"Yes, it does seem so, and I didn't even know where it was until you told me. When I read it on the back of the photograph, I thought it was a woman's name. Have you ever been there?"

Anna smiled. "Yes, quite a few times, many years ago with my grandmother. I must have been in my teens or early 20s. Then her health started to deteriorate. I believe she only went there twice more after that. The journey became too much for her. It really is a special place. I feel sure that you must own it. I don't think it was ever sold, so it must be part of my grandmother's estate."

"I will ask Mr Stone to check it out. Do you know of a property called Castilion?"

"No, never heard of it. Why?"

"Well, it seems I do own that – apparently, it's close to San Francisco in California."

"That's fantastic," Anna beamed. "Will you go there?"

"Oh, I doubt it," Tom replied.

"Why not?"

"I've never travelled very far. I know it sounds silly, but I'm 44 years old and I've never been further than Bournemouth. I went there with my mother when I was seven, but there's never really been a reason to go anywhere else. But if it turns out that I do own Ka'Lani then you are welcome to go there. As long as it's still fit for habitation, of course."

"Thank you, but I have plenty to do here for a while," Anna replied.

Tom finished his coffee and got up. "I must go," he said.

"OK, but do come back soon so that we can finish reading these. Shall I pick you up for the board meeting on Tuesday?"

"That would be helpful, as I don't know where I am going. You can keep those here for the time being," Tom said, pointing to Emily's letters.

"Thank you, and thanks for helping me through a difficult day."

"No problem, I enjoyed it. I'm also glad that we are able to talk and that you don't seem to see me as the enemy."

"I'm sorry, Alex has a way of making everything feel

confrontational. I was pretty hurt when my grandmother's will was read, but I've never blamed you."

Tom smiled. "I'm glad and I'll see you on Tuesday. Goodnight."

Chapter Nine

Living a Lie

The next morning, as Tom made tea and toast, he noticed how cold and empty the kitchen felt. He had a strong desire to go somewhere and see people, but he decided he had bothered folk enough for one week. It was raining, and with gardening out of the question, he resolved to do some more sorting. The bookshelves in the sitting room were his first target. He began by removing about ten books at a time, which he individually cleaned before wiping the gap they'd left on the shelf and putting them back. He was just finishing the third shelf when he heard a car pull up and someone rap on the back door. It was Anna. She looked pale and upset. "I'm so sorry to bother you, but I had to go somewhere," she said.

Tom offered her the chair, but once again it was piled with papers and rubbish from the desk. "Sorry about the mess, I'm trying to clear up," he said. "Let's go through to the sitting room."

Anna sat down in the big leather chair, unaware that she was the first person to visit that room, other than family, for as long as Tom could remember. She composed herself and began to explain. "Helen has been on the phone. She took

Jim, her husband, to get the car this morning, only to find it on a private driveway. They knocked at the house and a woman answered. She said she didn't know Alex but that it was her husband's car. She went back into the house to get him, and ... and..." Anna was becoming breathless.

"Don't tell me, it was Alex. Am I right?" said Tom.

Tears got the better of her. "He's been lying to me all along – he's married! I really believed he cared about me. We've been together for five years!"

"So, what happened next?" Tom asked. He wasn't surprised by the situation so far.

"Well, Alex could hardly tell more lies, what with Helen and Jim standing there. He said he would come to the office tomorrow. Helen told him that it wasn't convenient but he could come at 2 o'clock on Tuesday – that's the board meeting. She insisted on taking the car and she's coming to Larkspur this afternoon. She says she has done some work on the accounts and can see exactly what Alex has taken. I had to get out of the house in case he turned up or called. Helen said she left him and his wife arguing on the doorstep – I just know he will try and contact me."

They sat in silence for a few moments as Tom waited until he was sure that Anna had finished. "OK, now listen. It's better to get all of this out in the open. There's no need to worry about Alex. You can stay here for a while – he will never guess where you are. I will come back with you to Larkspur later and wait with you until Helen arrives, so you won't be on your own.

"She's coming at 3 o'clock. If I can go back for then I'll be fine. You're a very kind man, Mr Dwyer, thank you."

"Well, it gives me something to do other than this cleaning."

"Yes, you've got your work cut out here, let me give you a hand."

Before Tom could object, Anna was dusting and polishing the piano. He continued to pile papers into plastic bags, which he took through to the kitchen. As he was walking towards the back door, he froze with a deep aching pain that seemed to reach the very core of his being. The sound of Für Elise rang out from the study, ripping away years of his life like layers of dead skin. They exposed the pain of his sister's passing. He returned to the study, where Anna was seated at the piano with her eyes closed. He sat quietly and listened without her knowing he was there. After a very competent rendition of Chopin's Nocturne, Anna's shoulders sank and she opened her eyes to see Tom watching her. He was transfixed by the way the sunlight was playing on her auburn hair, and how a branch, flickering in the breeze, cast running shadows over the piano keys. Tom decided that without a doubt, Anna was as beautiful as her grandmother. "No one has played that piano since my sister Ella died," he said.

"Oh my goodness, I am so sorry, I..."

"No, no, it's fine," said Tom. "You play beautifully."

"What happened to her?" Anna asked softly.

"She was knocked off her bicycle and killed on her way to work. She was a primary school teacher in Downfield ... only twenty seven."

By now, Tom was almost in tears. He hadn't spoken those words for so long.

"That's dreadful," said Anna. "I remember reading about the accident in the paper, but I didn't realise that was your sister."

"Yes, it was a pretty awful time. I still miss her. Our mother left when we were very young, and so we looked out for each other – we were best friends. I tried to be the protective older brother, but I couldn't be on that day. Suddenly she was gone." Tom's eyes welled up again.

"I can relate to that," said Anna. I was very small when my parents died and didn't really know what was happening, except that I never saw them again. My grandmother was my parent and my best friend. I was schooled at home, so I was quite a solitary child. As my grandmother became ill, I began to realise how alone I was going to be. Then along came Alex. He was suave, debonair and confident, and he told me all the time how beautiful I was. When Grandmother died I felt so alone and he became my rock. Snap, the trap was shut!"

"Dad's health started to deteriorate after Ella died," recalled Tom. "In fact, he never really worked again. His arthritis got worse and he was depressed. Then he developed heart complications."

"What did he do when he worked?" Anna asked.

"He was a freelancer I guess. He couldn't get a full-time job after he left your grandparents' employment, so he ended up doing farm and estate accounts, and bookkeeping, for several people, mostly cash in hand. He managed to make a living from it. Jack and Laura were the first people to use him."

"And what about you, what do you do? You work at Glebe Farm too, don't you?"

"Yes, I am the farm manager, so I do paperwork and accounts, plus the day-to-day jobs that keep the place running. There's a large milking herd of Guernsey dairy cattle and Jack also has about fifty head of beef over at

Martlock, plus some odd bits of arable – mainly cattle feed, maize and the like. I manage the men and occasionally, when they are short, I get to do some of the general farm work. I quite enjoy that. Jack was brilliant when Dad got ill and he let me start later so that I could get him sorted out before I left. That's a big thing on a dairy farm!"

Tom realised that he was rambling. He hadn't talked to anyone like that for so long. "Hey, look at the time – it's two thirty," he said. "Better get you home."

Tom followed Anna's car in the pickup. He was determined to ensure sure that Dyson didn't cause her any trouble while she was alone.

When they arrived, Anna showed Tom into a room he hadn't seen before. It wasn't books that lined the walls this time, but paintings and photographs. Another large fireplace occupied most of one wall. There were photos of Emily when she was much younger, and some of Anna as a little girl with a man and a woman who must have been her parents. Tom noticed how there were no pictures of Emily's husband.

Anna placed tea on a table and seated herself in front of the fireplace, where a fire had been neatly set but not yet lit.

The doorbell rang. Anna stiffened and looked anxiously in its direction. Tom followed her out into the hallway, where she gingerly opened the door.

Helen Hobbs was six foot tall with shoulder length, blonde hair. She was in her early 50s and created a striking presence. "I'm so sorry, darling, you must feel dreadful," she said, giving Anna a hug.

In turn, Anna introduced Tom. "He's been a real friend over the last few days, and he has an interest in this as a board member."

Helen looked at Tom and paused for a moment. Then her face beamed with an openness that Tom immediately liked. She held out her hand as she greeted him. "It's so good to meet you, thanks for taking care of Anna. I met your father a couple of times – he was a good man." She turned back to Anna. "Now, darling, Jim and I have it all sorted. You are coming home with me for a day or so, until we have this situation dealt with."

"No," said Anna firmly. "I am not letting that man drive me out of my home."

"I knew you would say that. Would you like me to stay with you?"

"You know me too well. I guess I would feel happier with someone here."

"That's settled, then. I did bring a bag just in case. Now, I have never spent so long in this house without being offered a drink!"

Anna smiled. "OK, I'm sorry, I'm not a good host lately. I have just made coffee. Would you like a cup?"

"Coffee? Well, I suppose that would do to start with."

Tom was beginning to feel a little awkward. He tried to make excuses and leave, but Anna intervened. "Before you go, I would like you to hear what Helen has found out about the finances. It's a company matter, so you should be aware of it."

Helen Hobbs took a file from her briefcase, sat back in the easy chair and placed it in her lap. "Well, I'm sorry, but the bottom line isn't good. If what I suspect is true, then the guy is an out and out thief. I want you to look at these papers and tell me which ones you've seen before."

Anna duly examined the authorisations for payments to

directors, effectively her and Alex. "I only know of two of these," she said, and her eyes filled with tears.

"Yes, I thought so," said Helen. "The little shit has forged your signature. What's more, he has also forged Christopher's." She turned to Tom. "Christopher Jenkins – CJ – is our company secretary and legal bod. He's a signatory."

It was now clear that Alex had been slowly draining money from the company over a long period. This financial year alone, he had already acquired £490,000, as well as his generous salary.

Helen continued. "You must speak to the bank first thing Monday morning and freeze your joint account. The board will then need to make a decision on Tuesday about how to proceed." She reached for Anna's hand. "I think we need to involve the police," she said softly.

Anna shook her head in reply.

Helen turned to Tom. "What do you think, Mr Dwyer?"

Tom thought for a while. "Well, as far as the money is concerned, we need to see how much he can repay immediately. If that doesn't amount to much, then yes, the police must be informed. But I think we have to tell them about his double identity anyway. I'm sorry," he said, looking at Anna, who was staring hard at the floor.

"You must do what is best for you and the company," she said, sounding as if she was accepting defeat.

"Actually, Tom's suggestion sounds like good common sense to me," said Helen. "If we can recover the money then that is the best outcome for the company – as long as he agrees to stay away. I mean, that house I saw this morning has to be worth more than half a million."

"What about his wife?" asked Anna, bringing a pause to the conversation.

"Well" – Helen took a deep breath – "if you really want to hear this?"

"I do."

"Mrs Marcus Hodge – Deirdre – seems like quite a tough woman, but the poor soul just dissolved when it became obvious her husband had been lying to her. He really wanted to come to the office tomorrow, but I told him Tuesday. I had no reason for this other than to let the bastard sweat. In two days' time, he can answer to the board."

Tom smiled over Helen's direct approach. Even Anna enjoyed the vision of her friend in full flight.

"When I said I was taking the car he was incandescent with rage," Helen added.

Anna giggled. "He would be – that car was his pride and joy."

"Well, he had a new BMW there as well, so he won't need to take the bus just yet."

Helen's feelings towards Alex were becoming clear, and Tom wondered what the relationship had been like before now. Without saying anything, Anna got up and left the room.

Helen turned to Tom. "The thing is, normally the company could cover £500,000 out of its reserves, but we are stretched very thin this year after buying into a big development in Oxford. Poor Anna, this must be so hard for her. Unlike the rest of us, who knew Dyson was bad news, she always thought the sun shone out of his backside. I had him sussed very early on. He even had the cheek to make a pass at me. Me! I soon put him right and he's been dismissive of me ever since." Helen looked thoughtful. "I'm still worried for Anna, though. Dyson is a bully and I feel she hasn't seen the last of him. I'm worried he's capable of violence."

"Really?" said Tom, but in truth he wasn't surprised.

He felt he could be straight with Helen and took Emily's last letter from the inside pocket of his jacket. He gave it to her to read, which she duly did before handing it back. "Well, well, that changes things a bit! You obviously haven't shown this to Anna?"

"No, I'm worried about how she will react."

"I agree, but I think you have to tell her, Mr Dwyer – I think it will help her cope. She may be angry at first, but the longer this goes on the more difficult it will be for her to understand."

Tom felt that there was an authority and wisdom in Helen's words.

"Do you know what The HANA Trust is worth?" she asked.

"At this stage, we don't have a clue. I may know more tomorrow when I meet with Baverstock and Lyle, my father's accountants and investment brokers. It's pretty amazing considering that a couple of weeks ago I didn't even know he still had a bank account."

Anna returned with some cups and a full cafetiere.

"Right, who's up for coffee?" she said, trying to put a brave face on.

Helen got up. "Hell, no, I need something stronger," she said and marched towards the cocktail cabinet where she poured herself a scotch. "Anyone else?" she asked, but both Tom and Anna declined.

Anna looked pale. Her eyes were red and she was shaking. Seeing her distress, Helen went to sit next to her on the sofa.

"My grandmother must be turning in her grave," she lamented. "I have been so stupid. She had him worked out – she knew he was bad news. I've let him walk all over me. She died thinking her granddaughter was a complete fool."

Tom disagreed. He knew that if Emily was watching from anywhere she would be more likely seeing shades of her own reflection and the infidelities she'd endured. She would know Anna's pain. "That's not strictly true," he said. "I think that you should see this." He handed Anna the letter from his pocket. Then he and Helen watched as she read. When she had finished, she said nothing, but grew tearful once more.

"I don't know all the details about The HANA Trust yet," Helen said, trying to reassure her, "but we'll find out more tomorrow."

Anna took a deep breath. "So what does all of this mean?" she asked.

"It means," said Tom, "that we are going to sort this out – all of it."

"I hate needing to be rescued like a little girl," Anna said.

Helen cut in. "We *all* need rescuing here. Christopher and I should have been more insistent about Dyson, and we should have picked up what he was up to with the cash. So it's not just you."

Tom decided to change the subject. "Now, who else is going to be at this meeting on Tuesday?" he asked.

Relieved, Helen got up to pour herself another drink. "CJ will be there, as well as Val Marshall, who is PA to Anna and myself. She will be taking notes. And of course, we have Alex, also known as Marcus Hodge."

Tom winced at the very mention of Alex's name. "Does he own shares?" he asked.

"No, but he is a paid director. That's my fault – I suggested it and the board agreed.

Helen continued. "Normally Anna would chair but under the circumstances..." she tailed off.

"Christopher should do this one," suggested Anna.

Tom was deep in thought. "So, who exactly are our shareholders?" he said.

"Well, you own 33%, Anna owns 40% and The HANA Trust Investments of Hawaii owns 20%. They are sort of sleeping investors. We very rarely hear from them and then only through their accountants," Helen explained. "In addition, I own 5%. That was paid to me by Anna's grandmother some time ago as an honorarium for some work I did for her. I think of it as part of my pension fund. Christopher owns 2% – those shares were given to him in much the same way. So it's pretty straightforward."

Tom made some brief notes. "So, between us, Miss Margesson and I own 73% of the shares. Is that right?"

"Yes, that is correct."

Tom thought for a moment. "That's a controlling interest, isn't it?"

"Together, yes." Helen was smiling.

"So, as long as we stick together, we control things?"

"Yes, so long as you agree. Of course, if you don't, then it is down to the rest of us to vote for one or the other."

"And this trust, how does it vote?"

Helen explained that they had never really shown their true colours. An investment management company called

Harvester managed their shares, and also had the authority to vote on their behalf.

Tom was surprised at how well he understood everything. "Well, I think it's time I was going home – I have to go to London tomorrow," he said. "I will see what I can find out about The HANA Trust while I'm there."

The day was drawing to a close when Tom left the two women standing at the door of Larkspur. As he drove away, he thought of so many questions he would like to ask the next time he saw them.

Chapter Ten

Colonial Collections

The morning was chilly and signs of the first frost hinted that the trusted warmth of summer was succumbing to the stealthy advance of autumn. Tom met Martin Stone at the station in time for the 9 o'clock train. The solicitor had booked them first-class seats and they were served coffee and a light breakfast on the journey, which took just over an hour. As they travelled, Tom updated Stone on the last few days' revelations. He also showed him Emily's last letter. Stone told Tom that his own father was now back at work part-time, and he confirmed that Jack Deacon had been to see him. He said: "My father's view is that Miss Aldridge is decent, but she has been under this man's spell for a while. He doesn't believe that she is dishonest, but we could all be wrong about that."

At Paddington, they went by taxi to South Moulton Street.

Baverstock and Lyle was a long-established firm of accountants and an investment house. Its age showed in its rather grand and formal offices, which had dark mahogany woodwork, brass fittings and engraved metal nameplates on every door.

They were met by Dora Cleary, who had been the regular contact of Tom's father. She worked on behalf of one of the partners, Bernard Lyle, and gave them a run down of what they had been doing for Tom's father. The list of investments they managed for him in the UK was substantial and amounted to in the region of twenty-seven million. It was mostly property and what they called Gilts, a kind of government bond, plus a number of blue chip investments that were seeing good returns.

After a while, Bernard Lyle joined them. He was a stout gentleman and was dressed in a pinstripe suit. Tucked in his waistcoat was a watch and chain. He got straight to business. "You see, Tom, The HANA Trust works through a company called HANA Properties Hawaii Inc.. Its main business of property investment is done in San Francisco. They are very keen to have contact with you, as you now own it lock, stock and barrel. You also have immediate access to it."

"Not quite," said Tom, handing Bernard the last letter written by Emily Margesson. When he finished reading it, Tom spoke again. "So, you see, the trust is really for Ms Aldridge, but it's in my control for now."

"That explains a lot," said Bernard. "I wondered why she hadn't left her granddaughter all that much."

Bernard went on to explain that The HANA Trust was largely the residual of the Margessons' business dealings that side of the water. Emily had inherited interests in sugar and coffee and been advised well about diversifying into property, mainly in Hawaii. "Mind you," said Bernard, "that husband of hers nearly drank and gambled it all away. He made a serious dent in it, but it seems that she got some good guidance when he died and managed to turn the whole thing around. We've not been involved for some time, but it was quite substantial. The company has a board of directors but its sole purpose is to grow the portfolio for the trust and see to it that the properties are managed. Your father kept a close eye on it for a long time, but lately it has been left to its own devices. Chance Moxford is the CEO and he manages things on a daily basis. You need to meet him, Tom, and soon. Their office is in San Francisco."

Tom wasn't at all keen on making a trip overseas. "Would he come here?" he asked.

"Yes, if you really wanted him to, but I think Moxford is a slippery character and it would be good if you could get an up-close look at the operation. His son, Chance Junior, is also a director."

Tom asked: "Do you know anything about a company called Harvester? They seem to vote on the Margesson Board on behalf of the trust."

"Yes, that's us. We just do proxy work on behalf of international corporations. We simply vote as we are advised to by the company. That is about all I know – you certainly have your hands full sorting this lot out. Your father knew it like the back of his hand. I used to meet him regularly, say four or five times a year in Oxford, but that stopped when he got ill and since then we have kept the UK interests ticking over through William Stone in Downfield. Have you met him?"

"No, not yet," said Tom.

"William is my father," Martin Stone interjected.

"Oh yes, of course," Bernard laughed. "I should have connected the name."

Dora had a more detailed conversation with Stone about probate and Tom was happy to leave that to them. He carried on his conversation with Bernard about his father and the investments in general. Apparently, Emily and his dad did everything they could to keep the information about The HANA Trust on the other side of the water. Bernard and William Stone were trustees, but until he became ill it was his father who had managed things.

Bernard was able to solve the mystery about the property called Castillion. "It's owned by The HANA Trust, Tom, one of the directors live there. Take my advice and get a handle on them quickly. Let me know if we can do anything to help."

Bernard Lyle said his goodbyes and Stone wrapped things up with Dora. In no time, they were back in the street hailing a cab for Paddington. Before catching their train, they went for lunch at the station's Hilton Hotel to discuss what they had learned.

"So, this estate is huge, Tom," Stone began. "It is rather beyond us so I am going to send what information I have to Dora. She is already dealing with HMRC on death duties – they have had it in hand for a while. A handsome list of property is being valued and the sale of two of these should cover them."

"Will that be enough?" Tom asked.

"Seems like it will be more than enough, but either way, you have a very substantial fortune."

"OK, so I need to ask you something. As it appears there is plenty of money, how would I stand if I wanted to get my hands on about £750,000 right now?"

Stone puffed out his cheeks in surprise. "Err, well, you can't really touch any of the money in the UK until we have probate and that is likely to take months. But as I understand it, you have immediate access to The HANA Trust. Why do you want so much?"

"For one thing, I need to stabilise Margesson Holdings," said Tom. "Also, the letters make me responsible for ensuring Miss Aldridge's back is covered – The HANA Trust is there for that purpose."

Stone took out his mobile and rang Dora. After a few minutes' conversation, he said his goodbyes and returned it to his pocket. "Dora says she can probably get that cleared tomorrow. Do you want it paid to Margesson Holdings?"

"No," said Tom. "I would like £500,000 paid to Miss Aldridge and I will deal with it from there."

"Tom, are you sure she is to be trusted? You are putting a lot of faith in her." Stone stared hard at Tom and it was clear that he wanted him to think carefully about this.

"I know," Tom conceded, "and it's unlike me, but I do have faith in her, and anyway, if we give her this we will soon find out if she is trustworthy, won't we?"

"OK," said Stone, but his hesitant tone revealed to Tom that he was still reluctant. "I will let Dora know."

They were back in Downfield by 3:30 and Tom found a call box and rang Helen Hobbs. He filled her in on the day and also let her know that the cash difference in Margesson Holdings could probably be covered.

"That's great news, Tom, have you told Anna?"

"No, not yet, so please don't – I'd like to tell her myself."

Chapter Eleven
Cornered

By the time Anna collected Tom to go to the board meeting, he was so anxious that he was pacing up and down the kitchen. With so much going over and over in his head, he hadn't slept well. Yesterday's meeting with Baverstock and Lyle and all of the possible outcomes of today's discussions would not let him settle. He had risen early to return Jack's pickup as promised and found himself all ready to go by 10 o'clock. Two hours is a long time when you are counting down the minutes. Anna arrived on the dot at midday, and Tom was on his way down the path before she could get out of the car. Today her hair was swept back and tied in a ponytail, which fell onto a dark business suit. Only her sunglasses and her pale complexion hinted at the pressure she was feeling. She tried to smile as Tom got into the car, but she was clearly not herself. She said very little until they parked in an underground car park at the office. Tom could see the Lamborghini that Helen had taken from Dyson in a space just a few yards away.

"Well, I'm dreading this," she admitted.

"I know, but just remember that he's the one who has done wrong."

Anna just shrugged her shoulders.

"I will make sure the company is fine," Tom continued. "I've spoken with Mr Stone and I have a plan. I'll tell you about it later."

Anna remained quiet and was clearly preoccupied.

The offices of Margesson Holdings were not what Tom had been expecting. They occupied the ground floor of a five-story office block at the end of Downfield High Street. They walked into a reception area, where Tom was introduced to Janet, who described her job as, "Telephone, tea, coffee, travel, reception and anything else they can think of." She was clearly a happy, bubbly kind of person and she had worked for the company for over 20 years. They went through a security door and into a general office space, where three people were working at screens. There were four more offices, a small staffroom and a boardroom. Tom had imagined something far bigger and with more people. He was introduced to Christopher Jenkins, who Tom guessed was in his late sixties. He had steel grey hair, an incredibly straight posture and was impeccably dressed in a three-piece suite. Tom suspected he had seen military service. CJ welcomed Tom and they completed some paper formalities about his admission to the board. Then Helen appeared and handed Tom a company mobile phone. "Anna thought you should have this," she said. "Val has just arrived and she will show you how to use it. Anna also asked us to fix you up with a company car if that helps. We have spares at the moment."

Tom laughed. "Thanks, but I am not the Lamborghini type."

"No," Helen smiled. "There's another car that one of our surveyors handed back when he left last week. The lease is paid up for another four months, so you might as well use it."

"Well, that would be really helpful until I get sorted out with something. Thank you."

"Don't thank me, it's more yours than it is mine," Helen said, her smile never leaving her face. "Val will give you the keys and I will take you down and show you it later."

Tom wanted to call Stone and was shown to a desk that wasn't in use. When he returned, Anna was sitting all alone in her office. Tom closed the door. "I need a word," he said.

Anna could hear the seriousness in his tone. "OK," she said, looking up at him.

"I have just spoken to Mr Stone and £500,000 is ready to be transferred to your account – I just need you to let me have the number. It's from The HANA Trust on account."

"Oh, no! Please don't give it to me," Anna said. "Look at the mess I have made already."

"But this way you can now put the books straight when you are ready – and you won't have to worry," said Tom.

"Fine, I get that, but you do it, not me. Just give it to Helen."

"No!" said Tom firmly. "You must do this as a way of taking back control ... it will help you feel more confident."

Anna was clearly not happy, but she gave in. "Oh, OK, if it must be that way then Helen will give you the number of my account," she said sharply.

Tom had never heard Anna react like that to anything. He was shocked but understood the pressure she was under and how Dyson had brought her confidence to an all-time low.

At that point, Christopher interrupted. "We should go through to the boardroom," he said. "Alex is here and he is making a fuss because he can't get past reception. I need to start the meeting before we get him in."

In the boardroom, Val Marshall was seated with her laptop next to Helen, who was calmly peering at papers over the top of her half-frame glasses.

CJ began. "OK, I am not going to formally start proceedings until after we have met with Alex. So this is actually a shareholders' meeting and will be on the record as such."

Christopher had no sooner spoken those words when shouting broke out and the door burst open. Alex barged in and threw his briefcase on the table, with Janet close behind. "I am so sorry," she said. "He pushed through as someone came out. He has been so very rude."

Alex turned on her. "Oh, sod off, you sanctimonious little cow. I have every right to be here – it's a board meeting!"

"Stop and sit down, NOW!" There was no arguing with Christopher's command.

Shocked, Dyson did as he was told.

Christopher continued calmly. "I am so very sorry, Janet, that was disgraceful behaviour, which the board will not accept. My apologies." Alex was about to speak, but Christopher turned on him. "Shut up," he said.

Another member of staff came and ushered Janet out of the room, and once again Christopher took control. "Right, now, firstly, this is not a board meeting, it's a shareholders' meeting, and unless I am mistaken, you are not a shareholder. But since you are here you can answer some questions for us, firstly about the misappropriation of company funds. We would also like some answers about your identity."

Alex looked towards Anna. "Are you going to let this kangaroo court do this to me? You know I haven't misappropriated anything. We agreed I was acting for you, right?"

Anna stared at him. "No, that's not right. I have seen the things that I am alleged to have signed and my pen never touched the paper. Where is the money, Alex?"

Dyson smiled. "Well, you little bitch!" He spat out his words. "Are you really going to say you didn't know?"

"I did know about two sums, but it seems that you have taken a lot more that I didn't know about. You have stolen from us. I'll ask again. Where is the money?"

Dyson sneered as he said, "Look, darling, you and I both know I had to take some decisions because these idiots were running things into the ground. I needed to make some proper investments for us."

Anna slammed her hand down on the table. "I knew no such thing – you have lied and cheated the company, just like you have lied and cheated me."

Christopher had heard enough. "Our records show that you have £490,000 of the company's money. How much of it can you pay back? Of course, I could hand the whole thing over to the police as a clear case of fraud, but I assume you would like to avoid that?"

"There is no case," Dyson snapped back. "The papers show that she approved those payments." He jabbed a pointed finger at Anna. "If I am going down, she is coming with me."

"Only if those signatures turn out to be genuine," said Christopher, "and I for one know they are not."

Dyson opened his briefcase and pushed several bundles of cash across the table. "Here, have it," he said, "you are all pathetic – that's all I have!"

Helen started counting the money, as Dyson got up. "Now I am out of here, and you can all go and..."

Christopher cut in. "The board may still choose to pursue action, so there are no guarantees. I for one feel we have no alternative but to report the identity fraud."

When Helen had finished counting, she said, "There is about £200,000 here."

"OK, what else have you got?" said Tom, looking Dyson straight in the face.

"Oh my god! Now I have to deal with the farm boy!" Dyson sneered.

Tom laughed. "Yes, and because I work on a farm I know what bullshit looks and smells like, and I have just witnessed a whole load of it. Where is the rest of the money? Where are these so called investments you made?"

"'Where are these investments?'" Dyson said, imitating Tom's voice. "If you knew anything you would know they don't always pay off. There is no more money. Now, isn't it time for milking or something? Shouldn't you be on your way?"

Once again, Tom laughed. "Well, I don't believe you, you have more somewhere. You are a liar and a thief and there's no reason in the world to believe that you are suddenly telling the truth now. As far as I am concerned, the police can deal with you."

"We'll have a board meeting later today and decide then what we are going to do," said Christopher.

"I am entitled to be present," Dyson argued.

"No, Mr Marcus Hodge, we don't have anyone of your name on our board," replied Christopher.

Dyson sniggered and glared at Anna. "And as for you, you disloyal little bitch, I'll settle up with you in my own way and in my own time. And just so that you know, I never loved you. In fact, I couldn't stand the sight of your stupid face. And as for that cow of a grandmother..."

Tom had heard enough. "For heaven's sake, get out of here!" he said.

"Don't worry, I have had enough of trying to help a bunch of halfwits," Dyson retorted. With that, he got up and stormed out of the room – straight into the path of Helen and two police officers. They escorted Alex away as he shouted a stream of expletives.

"We need to take a break," Christopher said. "Has he definitely gone?" he asked Helen.

"Yes, but the police were only here responding to a call Janet made when he was kicking off earlier on, so I don't think they will keep him. I've not told them anything else."

"That call was over an hour ago," said Tom. "Good job he wasn't holding Janet at knifepoint!"

"Quite," said Helen, "but in a way good timing to get him off the premises."

They went back over what had just happened. After about ten minutes or so, Anna got up. "I need to clear my head, I'm going out," she announced.

I'll come with you," said Tom. "Just to be sure he's gone."

As they walked across the reception area, Anna was about to speak to Janet, when, unnoticed by her, a tall, blonde woman approached and hit her square in the face with a closed fist. The force of the blow almost knocked Anna off her feet.

"You filthy little tart! Couldn't find a husband of your own so you thought you could take mine, did you? Well, you are welcome to him." The woman proceeded to empty a bag of laundry over the floor. "This comes with him!" she spat. "You have no idea what he's like, but you deserve all you get."

With that, she stormed out. Anna ran back to her office, with Tom and Helen in hot pursuit. She slammed the door before either of them could enter. "Just leave me alone, all of you!" she shouted as the door slammed shut.

Anna's reaction was no great surprise to Tom or Helen – she had been incredibly well controlled throughout this whole business, and it was obvious that it would boil over at some point. They decided to leave her be for a while. Tom sat and discussed the board's recent history with Christopher some more.

"Dyson is a thoroughly bad lot if you ask me, but Anna wouldn't hear anything bad about him," Christopher commented. "We have all tried."

Tom now knew that both Christopher and Helen cared for Anna a great deal and had tried to protect her.

After an hour or so, Helen came in. "I'm worried," she said. "Anna isn't picking up her mobile or her home phone. I know she is mad with us and is feeling embarrassed, but I can't help but panic. I think I'm going to check if she has gone home. God knows where Dyson might be."

"OK, I'll come with you," said Tom.

"It's an opportunity for you to try that car," said Helen.

They went down to the garage and Helen showed Tom a Mercedes. "What?" he said. "I can't drive that!"

"Of course you can. Get in and I'll show you."

Actually, Tom had driven Jack's old Merc plenty of times and this proved no different, just a lot newer.

They drove out into the Downfield traffic towards the village. Tom quickly got the hang of things and was beaming until he remembered Anna's situation. "I'm worried about her, too," he admitted.

"If we find her we might get another mouthful," Helen warned.

"I don't care," said Tom. "At least we'll know she is safe."

Chapter Twelve

Touch and Go

As they turned into the drive at Larkspur, they could see Anna's car in the turning circle. The front door of the house was wide open.

In the hallway, Helen shouted for Anna but there was no reply. The sitting room and kitchen were empty and undisturbed. As she began to climb the stairs, Helen called again – still no response. Then she suddenly called out Tom's name and he bounded up the stairs, taking two steps at a time.

As he reached the top, he could see a breakfront dresser on the landing. It had been pulled over onto its front and the contents had all smashed onto the floor.

Helen gently pushed open Anna's bedroom door, calling her as she went. There was no one inside, but more furniture had been pulled over and the drawers had been emptied out onto the bed.

The silence was broken by Helen shouting, "Oh, no, Tom!"

Anna was sprawled out on the floor of her en suite bathroom. Blood from an open wound on her head was pooling on the grey marble floor. There were also spatters of blood on the shower screen. Helen knelt next to her and touched her hand. Anna was unconscious and cold, but her friend could detect a faint pulse; her complexion was marble grey, almost matching the floor. Tom grabbed the bedside phone and dialled 999. He threw Helen a blanket and she quickly covered Anna with it to keep her warm.

In what seemed like an age, but was probably no more than 20 minutes, the house was teeming with paramedics and police. Anna was rushed off by ambulance and it was hard to get anyone to say how she was. Tom eventually managed to get a paramedic to tell him that she was alive, but he could find out no more.

As the ambulance pulled away, another car swept into the drive and a woman got out and surveyed the scene. She made a short call on her mobile and walked towards the house. Tom weighed her up and decided the last thing they needed was a bloody reporter, so he decided to get rid of her.

"Yes? Can I help you?" he asked sharply.

The woman looked Tom straight in the eye. "And you are?" she said.

"Never mind who I am. We don't need you here – there's no story to be had so clear off and let the police do their work."

"Well, thanks for your support, sir," the woman replied, showing Tom an ID badge. "Detective Superintendent Marsden, Valley Police. Now, you are again?"

Tom swallowed hard. "Err, Tom Dwyer, I'm a friend of Miss Aldridge. I am sorry, I thought you were..." he broke off.

"Don't worry, Mr Dwyer, I'm glad to know that someone

is looking out for interlopers. Don't leave yet, please, we will need to speak to you."

Tom was keen to get to the hospital, but he realised the police weren't going to let him or Helen go anywhere until they had been questioned. He kept asking for an update on Anna's condition, but no one was saying anything. Both he and Helen gave their statements and provided a full account of the afternoon, including Dyson's behaviour. However, the police seemed to be treating it as an accident and believed Anna may have fallen after wrecking the place in a fit of pique, as nothing appeared to be missing. Tom knew in his heart that this wasn't true and he shared his concerns with Superintendent Marsden, who simply raised an eyebrow and said they would follow up all possibilities.

When Tom and Helen eventually arrived at the hospital, they found that no one would tell them anything, as they weren't relatives. When they explained that Anna had no living family, they were finally taken seriously. Dr Sophie Gallimore was the consultant in charge of her care.

"Will she be OK?" Helen asked, getting the most difficult question out of the way first.

Doctor Gallimore was gentle but firm. "We really don't know at this stage. She has received a number of blows to her head. The next twenty-four hours are critical and we hope to see some improvement in that time. We'll review her again tomorrow, but for now it's a waiting game."

"If she is OK, will she be left with any permanent damage?" asked Tom.

"I'm afraid there is really no way of knowing that yet. The human body is an amazing thing, Mr Dwyer. I have seen people make a full recovery from serious head trauma, but for now we need to monitor her, and it's a waiting game."

"May we sit with her?" asked Helen.

"Yes, please do, and talk to her, too. We find this often helps. She can probably still hear you. I will take you to see her, she is breathing independently but we are watching her closely."

Tom and Helen sat with Anna for a couple of hours, along with a young police officer, but she showed no signs of consciousness. Superintendent Marsden also came to speak to the doctor. She told Tom that based on three head wounds, they were now clear that Anna had been attacked. She asked more questions about Dyson and was keen to speak to him and eliminate him from her enquiries. Helen referred her to Christopher, as he had Dyson's address and other personal details written down. Once again, Tom and Helen gave their individual accounts and opinions about Anna's ex.

Helen prompted Tom to go home and get some rest. She vowed to stay with Anna for a while longer. He reluctantly agreed and said he would be back later. Once at the cottage, he wished he had stayed at the hospital. He made himself some food but couldn't eat it, so he washed and changed and headed back to the intensive care unit.

Helen was flicking through a magazine next to Anna's bed. She told Tom there had been no change and he urged her to go and get a break. "I will be fine here, honestly," he reassured her.

Helen gave Tom her mobile phone number and said she would be back in a few hours. It was already ten to nine in the evening. Tom sat in the easy chair next to the bed and looked at the sleeping figure motionless by his side. He reached out and gently touched Anna's hand, but he quickly checked himself and looked at the monitors that bleeped away by the bed and the drip that was slowly draining the bag of saline. The attending police officer had changed and a fresh-faced young constable had taken up the position outside the door. He had specific orders to call the station as soon as Anna regained consciousness.

Tom tried to quell his feelings of rage towards whoever had done this to Anna. He hoped that the police would arrest Dyson soon and he felt deep feelings of protection towards the granddaughter of his father's lover.

Don't let yourself get too close, Tom Dwyer, you will get hurt, he told himself over and over. His ever-present caution was showing itself true to form.

The day shift changed to the night one and a new nurse popped in every 20 minutes or so. Tom began to feel his own eyes closing and he drank coffee and read a two-day-old newspaper to try and stay awake. At 6am, Helen returned with some basics for Anna – a dressing gown and some toiletries – in the hope she would be up and around soon. Tom returned to the cottage, this time sleeping soundly for about four hours until he was woken by the sound of his new mobile phone ringing. He had only just learned how to make calls and had no clue how to answer them, but somehow he managed.

"Hi, Tom, it's CJ. How are things?"

Tom explained and said they hoped to know more a little later. Christopher informed him that the police had been searching for Dyson and had come up with some interesting facts. He said he would meet Tom and Helen at the hospital at about two, to bring them up to speed.

Back on Anna's ward, Tom crept quietly into her room. Helen had dozed off in the chair and there was no change in the patient. About ten minutes later, one of the monitors started to beep and Anna's eyes flickered. She began to make sounds, as if she was trying to speak.

Helen woke up suddenly, grabbed Anna's hand and started to talk to her. A nurse appeared and took over from her by calling Anna's name. In response, Anna opened her eyes. She looked terrified and the nurse explained to her that she was in hospital and called for Dr Gallimore. Tom and Helen left the room to give the medical staff more space.

After half an hour or so, Dr Gallimore appeared in the visitors' room to speak to them. "She is conscious, but at the moment she's very confused. That's quite normal and I'm not worried about it. The initial signs are good, but we are still at a critical stage and not out of the woods yet. I have asked for another scan, which may tell us more."

Tom and Helen felt sure that Dr Gallimore knew exactly what she was doing, and they trusted her judgement. They stayed in the small visitors' room and waited for Christopher. He arrived with two cups of strong coffee, which he knew would be very welcome. Tom and Helen updated him and after their coffees they went together to the hospital canteen for some food and a further catch up.

"It seems our friend Alex Dyson, alias Marcus Hodge, doesn't even exist!" said Christopher.

"Well, we knew that from meeting his wife yesterday," said Helen, who felt Christopher had just stated the obvious.

Christopher smiled. "Yes, but prints taken from Larkspur, his office at Margesson Holdings and the Lamborghini confirm that he is actually Timothy John Welland. He is under investigation for investment irregularities and disappeared from his original place of work in The City about five years ago, when his crimes were discovered.

"It would seem he has yet another wife and two children

in Hampstead, but they haven't seen him since then either. The police have a full manhunt in progress. They are still not completely convinced that he is the one who attacked Anna, but they are keen to find him.

"Now, I have seen his credentials as Alex Dyson, including a passport when we registered him as a director. We also have his bank details under that name. It would appear that he is using cleverly forged documents."

"Oh my God!" said Helen. "Poor Anna has been well and truly taken in!"

"And so have we," added Christopher. "This man has clearly been running a double – even a triple – life.

When they returned to Anna's room, she wasn't yet back from her scan, but Superintendent Marsden had arrived.

"Have you found him?" asked Christopher.

"No, not yet, but the picture is getting clearer all the time. The National Fraud Squad have a marker on him and they are very interested in recent events. They will need to speak to you."

Dr Gallimore arrived and said that Anna was still not fit to be interviewed, so Marsden left.

When Anna came back from the scan, Helen and Tom were allowed in to see her.

"They tell me you two have been my guardian angels," she said in a weak voice. "You've been sitting at my bedside and you came to find me. I don't want to think what might have happened if you hadn't done that. I still don't really remember what happened. Did I fall?"

Neither Tom nor Helen wanted to answer that question, not now anyway.

"They are still figuring that out," said Tom.

Anna drifted off into a deep sleep. The nurses reassured Tom and Helen that she was OK and would need to rest for a while, but they were welcome to stay. Helen said she needed to go and sort some things out at the office, but Tom was more than happy to remain at the hospital. He was so happy that Anna was OK and all thoughts of being tired left him. The sense of relief was enormous and he was grateful to everyone and everything. Although he was not a churchgoing man, he did not actively disbelieve, and he said a thank you in a silent prayer.

He sat with Anna as she slept in what Tom decided was a peaceful way. He stood up, walked over to the window and watched the people outside going about their everyday business. It had started to rain and the sky showed that more was to come as the afternoon drifted into evening. As Tom watched the ambulances arrive and depart, he suddenly heard Anna's voice behind him. "Hello, are you still here?"

"Yes, I am," said Tom, rushing to her bedside.

"Could I have a drink of water please?"

"Err, yes, but I'd better just check first."

Tom called for assistance and two nurses arrived. He left the room as they made Anna more comfortable and gave her some orange squash to drink. When he returned, Anna was sitting up and looked a little more like her old self. She was pale and her eyes had dark rings underneath them, but she managed a smile.

"How are you feeling?" Tom asked.

"I have a splitting headache and feel rather stupid, not to mention confused," Anna said. As she spoke, tears welled up in her eyes.

Tom wanted to reach out for her hand, but he resisted the

urge. "Now, don't worry about anything," he said. "Just concentrate on getting better."

"Why are the police here?" Anna asked, after spotting the constable.

"They are just trying to sort out what happened to you," Tom said, and Anna began to softly sob.

Another police officer arrived and introduced herself as DS Andrea Lucas. She politely asked Tom if she could speak with Anna alone, and so he went off to call Helen and Christopher.

After a few minutes, DS Lucas left and Tom returned to Anna, who was drying her eyes. "Oh God, what a mess," she said.

"Do you remember anything?" asked Tom.

"Alex turned up," Anna explained. "He was so angry. He said that he had been humiliated by the board and forced to pay back money, only to then discover The HANA Trust was giving me £500,000. He was in such a rage he started smashing things. How did he know about the HANA money, Tom? He seems to know everything. I told him I didn't have anything, but he reiterated that the money was being transferred today. I remember him hitting and shaking me, but nothing else."

She cried and Tom tried to console her, but he felt so helpless.

"The police say they are searching for him and they want to speak to him about this and a string of other things. Oh, Tom, this is all just awful. What a mess!"

Tom was shocked. This was the first time Anna had ever used his Christian name. "I don't know how he knew about the money, but I will find out," he said soothingly. "You can be sure of that. And at least now you are on the mend."

Helen arrived and gave Anna a huge hug as she sobbed and repeated what she had said to Tom.

In turn, Helen summed things up in her inimitable fashion. "Well, darling, don't worry, they will get the bastard and when they do I hope they cut his balls off, lock him up and throw away the key – the thieving little shit!"

As Helen spat out her judgement and sentence, Anna smiled and then cried again.

Through her tears, Anna apologised for the way she had behaved at the office. "I should have listened to you and CJ. You both told me he was bad news."

Helen smiled. "Yes, but love is blind, so don't worry. I don't blame you."

Helen and Tom were just relieved that Anna was showing signs of making a good recovery.

Chapter Thirteen
New Horizons

Anna continued to make a good and full recovery and after ten days she was allowed to return to Larkspur, where the security arrangements had been improved substantially. New locks and security cameras had been installed, as well as several panic buttons, which were dotted in various places around the house. Dyson still hadn't been apprehended, but he was believed to have left the area and the police continued to look for him further afield.

Tom went to see Anna on the day she arrived home, after not seeing her for a few days. He'd decided to try and create a little distance between them, as he was worried he was getting too close. Meanwhile, he'd been spending a lot of time at Margesson Holdings and learning about the company. He now knew it was mainly a property and lettings business, covering several areas, including Oxford and London. It even owned the building that its own offices occupied, and simply let out the other floors. Tom spent a full day with Stone and Dora from Baverstock and Lyle, which led him to take another big decision, which so far he hadn't shared with anyone.

When he arrived at Larkspur, Nora answered the door and gave Tom a cheery smile. "Hello, Tom, Miss Aldridge has been looking forward to you coming."

As he stepped into the now familiar hallway, he stared once again at the painting of Emily Margesson. He still felt that her eyes were drilling deep into his soul. Then Anna appeared. She had a broad smile on her face and looked the picture of health.

"I thought I was visiting the sick, but you look healthier than I do!"

"I am fine, honestly," Anna said.

Nora was clearly less convinced, and as she left the room, she said, "You need to rest, miss, these things take time."

Anna smiled. "Bless her, she's been fussing over me all day and treating me like a porcelain doll."

"Well, you have been through the mill a bit. It's only just over a week since we weren't sure if you were going to come out of this," said Tom, as he remembered with a shudder the last time he was at the house.

"You don't have to rush off, do you?" Anna said. "Because I thought I would take you out for dinner, to at least start saying thank you for all you've done."

"Well, maybe you should wait a day or two before you start running around like that," said Tom.

Anna looked him straight in the face. "Look, if I have learned anything over the last week it's that this is not a dress rehearsal. This is the only life we get and we must get on and savour every moment."

Tom couldn't really argue with that. "OK," he said, "but an early dinner."

Anna smiled and quickly posed the next question. "Where would you like to go?"

"I don't know," said Tom. "I think The Bell does nice food."

Anna laughed. "A pub? Oh, come on. Under the circumstances, I think we can do better than that. What sort of food do you like? French, Chinese, Italian, Indian?"

Tom took a deep breath. "Well, what's your favourite?" he asked.

"After ten days of hospital food, something spicy would be my choice. So how about Indian?"

"OK," said Tom, with slight hesitation.

"Great," Anna said, "as long as you like Indian food, of course?"

Tom said nothing and Anna noticed his reticence. "Ah, maybe you don't?" she enquired.

"Well, err," Tom hesitated again.

"Oh my God! You haven't tried Indian food, have you?"

"Well, not as such," Tom replied with a smile.

"Right, well, just trust me, this meal will change your life." She immediately picked up the phone to book the restaurant.

They drove to a building that Tom had passed many times. He'd often noticed the man in traditional Indian dress standing at the front door. The Spice Merchant was an amazing place with lavish décor, plush furnishings and several elephant carvings, which added a very Indian feel to the ambiance.

The tables had been set with crisp white damask table linen, with the napkins folded into roses. Tom decided that this was, without doubt, the poshest restaurant he had ever been to.

After starting with poppadoms and pickles, Anna ordered

a range of dishes, which Tom carefully sampled; chicken Madras, Chana masala, chicken tikka masala and plain rice with naan bread. Tom absolutely loved the chicken tikka masala, the rice and the bread, but he hated the chicken Madras, which almost took his breath away. Anna giggled as he swilled cold water, which only made things worse. They laughed and talked generally about the business, without mentioning Dyson at all. Then Tom told Anna that he had come to a big decision. She paused and the smile left her face. She knew Tom well enough by now to know that this was going to be a serious matter.

"What is it?" she asked.

"Well, life is very different for me now and although things are still a bit upside down, I've decided to tell Jack and Laura that I won't be returning to work. I think they already know it, but I feel I need to say it properly. I've talked it through with Mr Stone and he agrees that it's the right thing to do. He also reckons there is plenty for me to be getting on with at the moment anyway. I'm going to give them the news tomorrow."

After Tom's revelation, they decided to have dessert. Tom liked the sound of the ice cream as a means of cooling his still tingling pallet. "That was amazing," he said as the waiter scurried off to prepare their final course.

"I am glad you liked it and I'm sorry about the one that was too hot," Anna giggled, "but it was just what I needed. I have always loved Indian food. One day I am determined to go there."

"Well, what's stopping you?" said Tom. "You should think about it."

"I'm considering getting away for a bit, but it won't be to India. I'm not sure it would be the right place for me at the moment. It's not a great destination for a single woman travelling alone."

"Well, I have to face up to doing some travelling at some point," said Tom. "I've been advised that I really do need to visit America and meet The HANA Trust people. Mr Lyle has been a trustee and he really wants me to go and see things first-hand. I'm not even sure I can do the flying."

"You'll be fine. Is it to California?"

"Yes, and Hawaii – it's just too much," Tom replied, shaking his head. "I asked Martin Stone to come with me, but he isn't able to get away. It's a hell of a long way to fly for the first time on your own. I might look into going by ship. Apparently, they do go to New York."

"That's crazy, Tom!" Anna said. "New York is East Coast – that's only about half way!"

Once again, hearing Anna use his first name felt comfortable and right. The waiter delivered their desserts and coffee. Tom immediately scooped up a mouthful of ice cream, letting it linger on his tongue and cool down his mouth.

"Look, this might sound crazy," said Anna, "but what if I came with you, just for support with the flying? I could do plenty out there by myself, so I wouldn't be in your way."

Tom struggled over how to respond. On one hand he wanted to say yes, and on the other he was worried about getting too close. "I'm really not sure I can do the flying," he reiterated.

In truth, he'd been thrown by Anna's suggestion and was panicking inside. A big part of him loved the thought of them travelling together. After all, it was about the only way he would have the courage to do it. But he knew in his heart that he was falling for Anna, which would only lead to him getting hurt. A woman like her would never be interested in him – their backgrounds were far too different. Despite himself, though, he wasn't exactly refusing her point blank.

Anna continued in her inimitable and enthusiastic way. "You can do it, honestly. Once you've taken off, it's no different to being on a bus or a train. In fact, it's quite relaxing. I would so love to see some of those places, especially Ka'Lani."

"Well," said Tom, "I checked and it is owned by The HANA Trust, so I guess I do own it."

Anna was so keen that Tom finally began to engage with the idea. "How long would we be on the plane?" he asked.

"It's about ten hours to San Francisco, so you could stop over there, and then about five on to Maui. I could get Janet at the office to book the whole thing. When do you need to go?"

Tom was clearly still very nervous, but he was warming to the idea. "Well, if I listen to Bernard Lyle, the sooner the better."

Anna was now clearly excited. "So, in the next two or three weeks?" she asked.

Tom heard himself say OK before pointing out that Anna hadn't touched her dessert. "What is it anyway?" he asked.

"Gulab jamun," she said, "try it." She took Tom's spoon, loaded it up and fed him.

"Whoa, that's fantastic!" he said, savouring the sweet-tasting, cardamom-laced treat. It was so good he almost forgot what he had just agreed to.

"I'll get Janet onto it tomorrow. I don't suppose you have a passport, do you?"

"No, you don't exactly need one for Bournemouth," Tom quipped.

"That's OK, we have a service that will expedite one for you in a couple of weeks ... three at the most. Now, I am going to need to go shopping – I think some new clothes are in order."

After the recent trauma Anna had endured, Tom was pleased to see her so animated.

The following day, Tom went into the office and called Stone to fill him in on his plans. His solicitor was pleased and agreed to update Dora immediately, so that she could line things up the other end. He advised Tom to get a good briefing from Bernard Lyle before he went anywhere.

Anna appeared in the office mid afternoon following quite a shopping trip. She brought in presents for the staff to thank them for their support and also to apologise for all they had been forced to put up with. She found Tom with his eyes glued to a copy of the previous year's annual report. "Wow, that's heavy reading," she said as Tom looked up.

"Well, it's not as bad as it was before CJ went through it with me," he said. "Now I can at least pretend to understand it."

"I have something for you," Anna said, handing Tom a large, flat parcel.

He opened it carefully. Inside was a beautiful brown briefcase. The embossed badge on the front read 'The Bridge'. Tom was momentarily lost for words. He looked at Anna, who was clearly getting as much pleasure from giving as he was from receiving. "I don't know what to say, this is beautiful – it's almost too nice to use," he said, while beaming from ear to ear.

"Well, I felt it was the least I could do."

Tom put the case to immediate use and placed all his papers inside it.

"It will be perfect for your trip," Anna said.

"Yes, it certainly will be, and you have reminded me that I also have some shopping to do. I haven't a clue what I am going to need and I don't even own a suitcase."

"Well, I could help you. How about tomorrow?" Anna suggested with great excitement. "Let's go to London."

"No, I think Oxford will do the trick," Tom replied.

By the end of the next day, he reckoned he'd spent more in one day on clothes than he had in the rest of his life so far. They had started at the gent's outfitters, where Tom expected to buy a couple of shirts and a new jacket.

"You need casual clothes, Tom," Anna argued.

"What sort?"

"I suggest some polo shirts."

The assistant pointed at a rail and before Tom knew it, four polo shirts were on the counter.

"Now, how about shorts?" said Anna, who was clearly only just getting warmed up.

"I don't wear shorts!" said Tom.

"Well, you will – it's very hot where we are going," Anna responded, adding two pairs to the growing pile of clobber.

Within two hours, they had visited three shops, spent a small fortune and had as many parcels as they could carry, some of which were now packed in a rather smart, roomy leather holdall.

"I can't see how I will ever get to wear that lot," said Tom.

"Well, we will see, won't we," Anna grinned.

Chapter Fourteen

Taking Flight

Tom became aware of the clinking of glasses and the rattling of crockery. The flight attendant was making her way down the aisle with glasses of orange juice. As she passed one to Tom, she asked, "Would you like champagne in that?"

Tom looked at his watch. It wasn't even 10am. "Oh, no thanks, it's a bit early for me."

"Oh come on, Tom, it's Buck's Fizz – a classic for breakfast." Anna was pulling up her reclined seat and reaching out for her glass. Tom gave in and decided to try it. He watched Anna as she straightened her hair and pulled on her shoes. The morning sun framed her silhouette as it streamed in through the cabin window. Behind her, Tom could see a vast plateau of white fluffy clouds. While Anna had been asleep for several hours, he'd felt too uneasy to properly rest. Considering this was his first ever flight, eleven hours up in the air certainly was a baptism of fire. He had to admit that business class was comfortable and there had been no real problems, but for the first few hours he'd found it difficult to release his grip on the armrests.

He didn't feel like watching TV, so he got down to some serious thinking, going back over the last couple of months and the changes in his life; the shock of his inherited money; his view of the world; even his view of himself. At times, he hardly recognised himself in the things he said and did. In his own quiet way, he was quite proud of himself, but that wasn't all. He had come to realise that there was one part of his new life that had brought him real pleasure and a sense of peace. Whilst that was all fine to begin with, it was starting to worry him, as he knew it couldn't go on. It had almost stopped him agreeing to the trip and now, as he looked at Anna again as she gazed out at the Pacific Ocean below, he knew he would have to deal with it ... he would soon have to tell her about his concerns.

"Look, Tom!" she said, pointing out of the window. "There's the Golden Gate Bridge."

Tom couldn't bring himself to lean across to look. The cabin crew were strapped in and he thought how he would soon be taking his first steps on American soil, or any foreign soil for that matter.

After they'd completed immigration, collected their bags and gone through customs, a skycap loaded their luggage onto a cart and pushed it to the taxi rank. Tom was amazed by how different everything was to home. He felt like a child on his first trip to the seaside.

The Sheraton Hotel was another world again. Anna took Tom's arm to stop him carrying his own bags and she came with him to his room to tip the bellboy, before having her cases unloaded in the room next door.

Alone, he sat on his bed and looked around him. The

room probably had more floor space than his entire cottage. He pressed a button on the TV remote and the set burst into life, showing CNN news coverage of a fire in an apartment block in Oakland. As he switched it off again, there was a knock on the door. Anna breezed in and inspected the room. "Now, Tom, do you want me to go away and let you sleep, or would you like to go out? I just can't wait to get out into this beautiful city – I love it!"

"Well, to tell you the truth, I could do with some food and some fresh air, then I might be able to sleep," Tom said. He had not enjoyed airline catering.

Anna took charge. "Well, this is San Francisco, it's coming up to lunchtime and I know just the place. Come with me."

The Buena Vista Café, on Fisherman's Wharf, was quite close to the water and just a short walk from their hotel. The café had been famous for decades and claimed to have invented the Irish coffee. It was homely and welcoming and served traditional American diner fare. Scrambled egg and American bacon with an English muffin hit the spot for Tom. Anna couldn't resist the eggs and bacon with American pancakes and maple syrup.

After they'd eaten, Tom admitted to feeling tired so they made their way back to the hotel, where Anna left him to rest. "I think I will have a walk around the shops," she said. "I'll give you a call about six. Try not to sleep for too long."

Two hours was all Tom could manage. Unable to get back to sleep, he decided to take a shower and change his clothes. He sat for a while drinking tea and watching the street below. In many ways, the activity taking place was the same as in any city street back at home, but in other ways everything was different – the clothes, cars, people and even their mannerisms. The sun was shining down on a perfect Californian afternoon and Tom could see the Golden Gate

Bridge standing in all its splendour across the water. Once again, he became preoccupied by the serious conversation he needed to have with Anna very soon. He vowed to do it that day.

Stepping outside into the heat of the late afternoon came as quite a shock after the air-conditioned Sheraton. Tom wandered along Fisherman's Wharf looking at the array of boats, seafood dealers and food stands. He watched as the dealers sold portions of chowder served in bread bowls made from a round sourdough loaf with the top cut off. He was amazed that the hot liquid didn't run through and that you could eat the bowl once you'd finished the soup. Seafood of every kind was on sale: shrimp, lobster, crab, scallop, scrod, blue fish and mahi-mahi from the Mid-Pacific. This all changed hands quickly and appeared to be available in endless quantities. Tom walked the length of the wharf and took in the sights before becoming aware of how late it was and how hungry he felt. He was glad to get back into the cool of the hotel lobby.

"There you are!" said a familiar voice behind him.

Anna sounded concerned. Tom turned to see her dressed in an oatmeal-coloured linen suit. Her red hair perfectly complemented the maroon blouse and matching hairclip she'd teamed with the outfit. She looked stunning. "I was hammering on your door for ages. I was getting quite worried."

"Oh, you don't need to worry about me," Tom said.

"Now, dinner. I've had a few thoughts." Anna's voice was full of her usual enthusiasm.

Suddenly, Tom felt himself retreating. "Well, I'm not sure."

"What about?"

"Well, to be honest, I'm not really hungry," he lied.

"What's wrong, Tom?" Anna asked, feeling that there was more to his reluctance.

"I just think it would be best if we left things for tonight."

"Why?"

"Well, I need to get some more sleep."

"OK, well then I guess it's room service and an early night for me, too." Anna sounded disappointed, but quickly recovered herself. "But Tom Dwyer, if you insist on standing a girl up for dinner then the least you can do is buy her a drink at the bar before you retire." She smiled as she gently teased him.

They made their way into the bar and Anna spotted the cocktail menu. "Oh, wow, I love cocktails, don't you?"

"Ah, well, err ... to be honest, I've never ..."

"You are joking?" Anna looked at Tom hard. "You really haven't had a cocktail before, have you?"

"No," Tom laughed, "I never have."

"Oh, come on, live a little!"

Anna ordered two strawberry daiquiris and they watched as the bartender made them in a very flamboyant and extroverted fashion, bringing the shaker up above his head and throwing it from hand to hand and up in the air, before catching it behind his back. After the show, he poured them into the glasses that had been set on the bar.

As they sipped their drinks, Anna described her afternoon shopping. Clearly she had enjoyed every minute of it. "I finally found this at Nordstroms," she said, stroking her new jacket. "I love this city. I took a cable car. You should do that tomorrow – you can't leave San Francisco without riding a cable car."

Tom drained his glass.

"Not so bad, eh?" Anna laughed.

"No, very pleasant. Shall we have another?"

As the waiter cleared three glasses from each of them, Tom and Anna both refused refills.

"Now, are you quite sure I can't tempt you to dinner? Last chance..."

"No, I would like to, but ..."

"But what?"

"Well, there are some things we need to get straight."

"What things?"

"We just need to talk and slow down a bit," said Tom, realising too late that cocktails were not for the faint-hearted.

"But at least you've got your smile back," Anna commented.

"I'm OK, really," Tom beamed. "I've just had to deal with so much change over the last few months, and I'm worried."

"OK, OK, it's obvious we need to talk. So why don't we do that over dinner?"

"All right," said Tom, "to tell you the truth, I am now starving, but it's on the condition I get to pay. You get to choose where. Nothing too fancy, though, I'm not in the mood for fancy."

"Delmonico's," said Anna emphatically. "It's not fancy but the food is fantastic and it's not far from here. We can walk there."

As they stepped out into the warm evening, Anna gently

took Tom's arm, but he tensed and pulled away. An awkward, embarrassed silence hung between them for a moment or two. "I'm sorry, Tom, it's just a force of habit."

"I know," he replied. "I'm sorry too. I didn't mean to react like that, I'm just very jumpy at the moment."

Anna thought for a while and then asked: "Is that why we need to talk?"

"Yes."

"OK," she replied cautiously.

Delmonico's was a small, dimly lit restaurant with an oak-panelled dining room and crisp white tablecloths. The waiters were dressed in full-length black aprons and waistcoats.

"It's just like how I remember it," said Anna. "My grandmother loved it in here. They used to treat her like royalty."

They ordered fillet steaks with all the trimmings and tucked into sourdough bread and salad as they waited for their mains to arrive. A recording of an Italian crooner sang his heart out to the accompaniment of a big band, and it seemed a perfect fit.

"So, am I in for a shock? Are you going to tell me that you're not Tom Dwyer after all?"

"No, nothing like that, though there have been times when I wished that were true."

"Go on."

"Well, just look at the last couple of months. My life has been turned upside down. Suddenly, I have money, financial responsibilities, excitement, and I'm flying off to new places. It's different for you. You've been brought up with this lifestyle, I haven't. I know life is never going to be the same again and I can deal with that, but I am struggling with myself. I don't recognise who I am anymore. I hear myself say things and can hardly believe it's me. There have been so many changes and I really wouldn't mind if some things went back to the way they were, but other changes go deeper."

"Like what?"

"Well, the old me would never have had a friend like you. I would never have sat in a posh restaurant on the other side of the world with an Anna Aldridge. Don't get me wrong, it's a wonderful thing, and I am as proud as punch to be here, but what will I do when this all goes away, when you move on? I am becoming too used to you being around and looking out for me."

"Me looking out for you? That's a good one. Who has been there for me all through this stuff with Alex? You have been a rock, Tom, and you need to believe it."

There was a pause, as the waiter served their steaks.

"I do understand, Tom, I really do, and to some extent I feel the same way, but I guess I have had more practice at reinventing myself. If I had to, I know I could do it again, though I really don't want to. I sort of did that when my mother and father died, and again when I lost my grandmother. Over the last few weeks, with Alex gone, I've had to start the process again. But this time it's different. I am doing it by myself, with your support, of course. You have become a good friend, Tom, and I would certainly miss you if you weren't here.

"You are right about one thing, though, if it weren't for

the money and the business we would not be sitting here, but that would be my loss, Tom – a big loss. Nothing needs to go back or stop, so let's just get on with now." Anna's voice had risen and she stopped to dab her eyes with a tissue.

Tom took his chance to make a point. "All that is fine, but look at it from my point of view. I've flown off to the sun with a beautiful woman, who I've come to care about, probably too much. Our friendship is the best bit of all of it, but we are very different and I can't change. I have to take stock or I will lose our friendship, mess it all up. After all, I've done it before."

"Oh, how?"

"I had a girlfriend – Audrey – she was an accountant at Sampsons. We went out together for five years. Dad didn't really like her, but I thought she was just about perfect. Then one day she went off with a fellow accountant who was a partner in a big London firm. I was crushed and life was awful for months. I can see that happening again. You and I come from such different backgrounds."

Anna's expression hardened. "You feel really out of place with me, don't you?"

"No, quite the opposite, but I know things will change. Your life will move on, mine won't. Not in that way ... I have to protect myself."

"Oh, OK, well that's that then, isn't it? It seems you think I'm that fickle. Are we having dessert?"

Anna chose strawberry shortcake with caramel sauce and Tom opted just to have tea, but he was learning fast that searching for a decent cuppa in the USA was possibly fruitless. They didn't speak much for the rest of the evening. Anna was clearly hurt and cross and Tom was unsure what to do next. He had expected to make a mess of the conversation and that's exactly what had happened. They discussed plans for the next day in a business-like fashion before walking back to the Sheraton.

Breakfast saw them both choose cereal from the self-service cart. They finished with coffee and toast and then the car arrived to take them to the banking district. Anna went off to look round some more shops, while the morning proved to be another avalanche of surprises for Tom.

Mr Chance Moxford was CEO of Hanna Properties of Hawaii Inc. (HPH). Originally from Texas, he was a large-framed, rough and ready businessman who was clearly focused and hard. He insisted on calling Tom Tommy and kept telling him they were going to be "such good buddies". Tom was certain that this was not going to be the case.

But the biggest shock came when Tom discovered the identity of the present tenant of Castillion. A name from the past suddenly surfaced like a jack-in-the-box, and he could barely take it in.

Tom heard Moxford's version of how well the company was doing and how there was no need to change a thing. He left knowing that many changes were indeed required. He had not liked Moxford one bit and what's more, he decided that he couldn't trust him as far as he could throw him.

He called Bernard Lyle and informed Moxford that he wanted to visit Castillion later that day. He then met Anna and they stopped for more coffee at Starbucks on Geary Boulevard. Anna ordered two vanilla caffe lattes, which Tom decided was one of the best things he had ever tasted. They laughed as he got milk foam on his nose and, as Anna brushed it away, she said, "Tom, I would be a fool to let this friendship fade away."

As they walked back along Geary, they saw that their chauffeur had pulled in further up the hill. Anna took Tom's arm once again. He flinched and then relaxed – it felt good.

"Sorry, force of habit," Anna said, and they both laughed.

The car took them over the Golden Gate Bridge and into Marin County. Tom looked at the forbidding sight of San Quentin State Prison and felt as cold as he had when Anna pointed out Alcatraz in San Francisco Bay. They continued their journey into Sausalito, where Castillion was located.

Chapter Fifteen

Missing Pieces

Still trying to take in the revelations of the morning, Tom was resolute that this next meeting was going to be just fine.

He pushed open a stiff iron gate and he and Anna stepped into a beautiful garden. Bougainvillea was in bloom everywhere and lemon trees bore ripe fruit and were surrounded by flowering cacti. The grass was well manicured and watered and had held its own against the Californian sun.

As they began to crunch their way along the gravel path towards Castillion's front door, they paused and looked at each other with apprehension.

"Come on," said Tom, "it will be fine."

A tall, imposing woman with jet-black hair and olive skin answered the door. Tom reckoned she must be in her late forties. "Good afternoon, ma'am, we are here to see…"

"Ah, yes," she said, cutting them off. "We are expecting you. Please come this way, the señor is by the pool."

She led the way through the tastefully decorated and

furnished house, which had clearly benefited from a woman's touch. French doors took them out into the garden again and onto a large, paved courtyard, where a blue pool rippled in the sunshine. Luxurious furniture was placed strategically around the water and a distinguished elderly man was seated on a sunbed in the shade. He tried to get to his feet but was clearly having difficulty.

"No need to get up," said Tom.

The old man sunk back down and allowed the woman to rearrange his cushions and make him comfortable again.

Tom hadn't seen him since he was eight years old and he could immediately see that the years had taken their toll.

"Sit down, please." He waved his hand at the empty chairs and Tom and Anna took seats at the table. "Conchita, please get some drinks for Mr Dwyer and Miss Aldridge."

The woman scurried away as the old man took a telephone call, turning away to speak in hushed tones. She returned with a tray of iced tea and glasses.

Tom took in the idyllic setting. He gazed at Anna as she sipped her tea and then closed her eyes, tipping her head back in the chair to let the sun play on her face. Her red curls were gathered loosely in a band and were spread over one shoulder. When she opened her eyes and caught Tom looking, she momentarily stared back and smiled. Their gaze was broken when the old man put down the phone and apologised for his temporary absence from the conversation.

"Well, Tom, that was Bernard Lyle. It seems that we have some talking to do. I always knew we would end up doing this."

At this point, Tom felt that he should say something, but he decided to remain silent and allow his uncle Al to search a little longer for words to fill the rather uncomfortable silence.

"I was sorry to hear about your father, Tom. I wanted to come to the funeral, but as you can see, I'm not fit to go far."

He turned to Anna. "My God, you are so beautiful, just like your grandmother. It's uncanny – your hair is exactly the same."

"Thank you, I take that as a great compliment." Anna beamed at being compared with her great hero and mentor.

The old man turned again to Tom. "You probably don't think much of me. I've been out of your life for too long, almost thirty-five years, but now that you are here there are things you need to know ... it's time to set the record straight, not just about the money and the business. That stuff is another matter and is largely down to your father anyway."

"I know that," said Tom. "I've had enough shocks and surprises to last a lifetime."

"But there is more that you don't know, and it's time you did."

Tom looked quizzically at his father's only brother. He could see no resemblance of any kind. "Oh?"

"Conchita, ask my wife to join us, would you," the old man called.

"Your wife? Well, well. Did dad know? He never said."

"Oh, yes, Tom, he knew."

At that point, time became suspended for Tom, as his mind and body were caught in the past as it tumbled over and over at the sound of a woman's voice behind him say, "Hello, Tom."

He felt thirty odd years of joy, pain, love, bitterness and longing tearing at his heart. The shock of his father's secret life had been hard to take, but this? This was a hundred times worse. This was the voice that had read him stories at bedtime, chastised him for throwing stones, reassured him when he was upset and sung him happy birthday every year for the first eight years of his life. He'd known immediately who the voice belonged to, and he'd missed it so much it hurt. It was the one he'd cried for weeks to hear again, and it came from the woman he'd blamed himself for driving away.

He could hardly bring himself to turn around. Anna was watching, and she knew what was happening. Slowly, Tom turned his head to see an elderly woman with a walking cane. Her radiance and the softness that he had known so well were still clear to him. Her face, although older, was familiar and he wanted to rush over and hug her. At the same time, he felt like shouting and asking why she had left them so suddenly, although today's visit had provided the answer. He couldn't bring himself to speak, as the tall, proud woman made her way towards him, leaning heavily on her cane.

Conchita helped her to sit at the table and poured her some iced tea. She looked directly at Tom. "Please don't hate me," she said. "We all made a dreadful mess of things."

Tom was barely able to think, but he heard himself say, "I certainly don't hate you. To be honest, I don't know what to think or feel. Life was never the same after you left, and then Ella..."

"I know. I wanted to come back to England so much, but I just couldn't bring myself to face it, and all of you. Your father took it badly, didn't he?"

"Yes," said Tom. "Ella's death changed him forever. What I just can't understand is why he didn't tell me anything about all of this business stuff. I was completely in the dark until a couple of weeks after his death."

Frances Dwyer smiled at Tom. "I am so sorry," she said. "We all tried to tell him that letting you know was the best way to go about things, but he just wouldn't listen. And once your father had made up his mind…"

"I know," said Tom. "I know."

Al Dwyer pulled himself forward in his seat and spoke directly to Anna, who had been sitting listening intently. "You see, Anna, the four of us made a whole bunch of big mistakes. We all ended up marrying the wrong people. John and Emily should have always been together and I should have been with Frances, but..."

"So, how did it all go so very wrong?"

"Well, for one thing, John felt it would be too hard on Emily to marry beneath her station, so to speak. I think she would have wed him in a heartbeat, but he thought her parents would take it too badly and that she would be cut off. Personally, although I think it would have caused some fuss, things would have calmed down eventually, but John wouldn't have it.

"Frances and I were together when we were teenagers, but we drifted apart when I went into the service. By the time I came home on leave, Emily was engaged to Victor and your father had proposed to Frances."

"I think he was just taking care of me," Frances interjected. "John and Emily never stopped loving each other, and in truth, neither did Al or I. But things were different in those days.

"I stayed with your father even after he was sacked from

the farm and when all the rumours were rife about his affair with Emily. But once you were old enough I decided to leave, and he didn't stand in my way. In fact, he asked Emily to set us up out here. I have no idea why he and Emily didn't get together in the end, but he could be a stubborn and intransigent person when he wanted to be."

"And that's the truth," added Al. "Over the years, John and I had many fall outs over business and money."

"When did the two of you last speak?" Tom couldn't resist asking.

"Well, I guess I spoke to him just before last Christmas." Tom was shocked – he thought his dad and Al had been estranged for years. "He used to call me from his lawyer's office. I was forbidden to write to him at the house."

As the afternoon passed, the heat drained from the sun and by four o'clock it was starting to draw in. They spent some more time discussing The HANA Trust and Al was interested to learn what papers there were on Maui. He asked Tom to let him know, but his nephew sidestepped the issue and ensured he didn't agree to anything just yet.

It was time to leave. As Tom and Anna bade their farewells, Tom gave his mother a hug that took him back more than 30 years. They promised to speak again once Tom was home and he vowed to get to know Frances better.

Back in San Francisco, Anna persuaded Tom to take a cable car ride. Darkness was setting in and the city lights were just beginning to shimmer – it was a sight Tom knew he would never forget.

Chapter Sixteen
Pineapple and Aloha

The flight from San Francisco to Maui was much different to the first one Tom had taken. It wasn't so grand or comfortable and yet this time he felt much more relaxed. Although he'd really wanted to see more of San Francisco, there was business to be done.

Anna was really excited about her return to Maui. "Tom, it's such a wonderful place, I can't wait to see it again," she told him mid-journey.

"What are you looking forward to in particular?" he asked.

"Seeing the house and the ocean. I had such happy times there. My grandmother spent a lot of time with me, playing and showing me things. When I was older, we were more like friends having an adventure together. It didn't feel like we were a grandmother and granddaughter at all."

The Maui experience began the moment they stepped off the plane. A group of musicians played Hawaiian music and a woman placed fresh flowers around Tom's neck while her colleague did the same for Anna. The offer of fresh pineapple completed the Maui aloha. Anna took it all in her stride and was clearly ready for it. Tom, on the other hand, was not. Anna watched and smiled as he soaked it all up, beaming from ear to ear. It was 1pm Pacific Time and the Hertz desk had their car ready and waiting.

They drove around the coast to Lahaina and went straight to the bank, where the manager showed them to a secure room inside the main vault. Two assistants produced a large box. Tom found the key and opened it. Both he and Anna were amazed to find it full to the brim with papers, bags and boxes. On top of everything was a pink envelope addressed to Anna. She recognised her grandmother's handwriting and slowly opened it before starting to read. Tom remembered how he'd felt when he opened Dad's box at the bank in Downfield.

Dear Anna,

I'm so glad this letter has found its way to you and wherever I am, in this life or the next, I will be hugely relieved to know that things are finally out in the open.

To begin with, please know that I love you so much and that I am immensely proud of you. I see so much of me in you and, of course, I will always see your mother in you. You will not recognise that because you hardly knew her.

I hope that John Dwyer is with you and has now revealed to you why my will was as it was. I know you will have been hurt and wondered why I left you so little, but I had to protect you. I know better than anyone how love can be blind. I believed that your grandfather loved me and his flattering tongue won me over. But I am sorry to say he was cruel and selfish. I found myself unable to do anything but make excuses for him and convince myself, and others, that he was a good man. He was not! Fortunately, I have been able to love someone with all of my heart unconditionally – someone who has really and honestly loved me back. I want to tell you there is no greater thing. By now I hope you understand.

If you have found Alex to be a good man and have married him then you have my blessing and my love. If things didn't work out then of course you still have my love and a chance to start again. I hope you have trusted John. He was the real love of my life and I was the love of his, but a mixture of circumstance and pride conspired against us. We were a brilliant partnership in business and much of the money was made by John after your grandfather died. Victor left me with a lot of debt and John cleared it up and advised me well. I regret every moment of every day we didn't spend together.

Don't fall into the same trap, my love. When you see that someone genuinely loves you unconditionally then do not waste a day of this wonderful life.

My love to you,

Grandmother EM

Tom began to sort through the box – piles of share certificates, more jewellery and about twenty bundles of hundred dollar bills. From reading the bands around them, he estimated it amounted to around $100,000. He looked at Anna, who was now weeping, with tears running down her cheeks. She walked over to Tom and handed him the letter to read. Before he could begin, she hugged him and sobbed hard into his shoulder, her cries coming from deep inside. Tom held her close, his own feelings churning over and over. This was the closest he'd been to a woman for five years. He wanted this contact with Anna so much, but he also wanted to reassure her and to make things right. That was his priority. She squeezed him tight and, when she finally let go, she dried her eyes, drew a deep breath and said, "OK, now what else is there here?"

They looked through piles of papers, around twenty more property deeds and land titles that appeared to have been purchased directly by Emily rather than through the company, as well as hundreds of share certificates.

"We'll need professional help with all this," said Anna.

"Yes, I agree, but it should stay here for now."

As Anna looked at the jewellery, she remembered her grandmother wearing it. And one piece, a large ruby ring, she knew to be her mother's. She picked it up and placed it on her finger. "The rest should stay here for safety," she said, "I don't want to lose that lot too."

A cigar box contained even more letters from John to Emily, and vice versa. There was also a large brown envelope packed with photographs. They placed them in Tom's briefcase to take away and look at later. They also opened an account in Tom's name and deposited the cash.

Although it was just coming into November, as they drove into Makena, the temperature was 84 degrees and the sun was beating down, unfiltered by cloud. They stopped outside a small clapboard house called Ka Hale Pua. It was the home of Mariah Smith, who had been housekeeper at Ka'Lani for years. She recognised Anna as soon as she opened the door and was clearly pleased to see her. Mariah was a native Hawaiian, five and a half feet tall and heavyset. Her black hair was tied back in a bun. "I've kept the place as decent as I can," she said, "but it's hard when no one lives there. Right now, it's all made up ready for you and Bartholomew is staying there so he can look after you. I will call and tell him that you're on your way up. It's really good to see you again, ma'am."

Anna gave Mariah a courteous hug and they left. Anna explained to Tom that Bartholomew had originally been brought to Maui from Barbados by her grandfather, Victor, to work as his cook and valet. He was also Mariah's partner. They were driving up an incline that was overhung by palms and heavily shaded from the sun. Eventually, they reached a wider track and a driveway, over which hung a sign that read Ka'Lani. They pulled in and parked in front of a classic colonial house, which was built with a mixture of clapboard and brick. The clapboard was freshly painted white and two large columns either side of the front door supported a balcony walkway that ran all around the property. Two rocking chairs stood to one side of the front door on the porch, whilst to the other was a swing seat covered in cushions.

"Isn't it beautiful, Tom?"

"It certainly is," he said.

Before they could knock, Bartholomew threw the door open and walked towards them. "Miss Anna, just look at you! You get more beautiful while I just get old and more ugly."

Anna gave the old man a hug, which clearly pleased him. She introduced Tom and led them into the house. It had looked colonial from the outside and colonial it certainly was. There was a very grand stairway, casement windows with rounded tops and huge brick and stone fireplaces. Each room was filled with antique furniture and paintings, and the polished wood floors were protected by thick rugs.

"Would you like tea, ma'am?"

"Oh, yes please, Bartholomew. Could we have it on the back porch?"

"Yes, ma'am."

Anna was almost giggling with excitement as she led Tom towards the back of the house. "Right," she said, "close your eyes and don't open them until I say so."

Tom did as he was told. Anna gently took his arm and pulled him outside. "It's OK to open them now," she said.

Tom gasped as he took in the most fantastic view of the shoreline and the ocean. He could see another island in the distance and mature palm trees lined the empty, sandy beach that outlined the crashing waves of the Pacific Ocean. They sat on a veranda, which had steps down to the beach, and drank tea while looking at more of the letters and photos.

When Bartholomew came to clear their cups away, he said, "Mariah has made up the master bedroom for you, miss, and the Clipper Room for Mr Dwyer – is that okay?"

"The Clipper Room?" enquired Tom.

"Yes, you'll see," Anna teased.

"Okay," he said, "Well, we'd better get our things from the car."

"Erm, I think you'll find that your things are already in your room," Anna said with a smile.

"Oh, err, OK," Tom said and got back to reading.

The letters were much the same as the ones they had read at Larkspur, except they were from an earlier time. Many of them were written while John and Emily were on Maui and clearly very much in love. Some of the envelopes bore no addresses, just names, and had clearly been written as part of their daily courtship, when they were also seeing each other regularly.

Anna read the letter from the pink envelope again, but this time with dry eyes.

After a while, Bartholomew came to ask what time they would like dinner.

"Not tonight, thank you, we're going out," Anna said. "You can go off now, we'll be just fine."

"Well, thank you, ma'am. What time will you be requiring breakfast?"

"How about 9 o'clock?"

"That's fine, and it's so good to see you again, ma'am."

"Thank you. It's good to see you too, Bartholomew."

"Oh, and Mariah said to tell you that 'they' are back."

"Oh, fantastic!"

Tom looked up from his reading. "What the heck was that all about? Who are 'they'?" He needed time to prepare to meet more strangers, but Anna just smiled in response.

They dined at The Pioneer, in a beautiful old building in the middle of Old Lahaina. The seafood was spectacular and they ate clam chowder for starters and large shrimps for their main. The service was excellent and Anna chose the wine, a white Zinfandel from California that was particularly good. After dinner, they strolled along the water's edge, where groups of locals were singing and dancing.

"It's a luau," Anna explained. "A traditional Hawaiian celebration."

They watched for a while as two Hawaiian women danced the hula. A tall, thickset man approached them.

"Hey, you two! Come and join us and have a drink. 'They' are back, you know!"

Tom and Anna excused themselves and continued on their walk.

"Who are 'they'?" Tom asked again. He clearly hated not knowing.

"You'll just have to wait and see," Anna replied mischievously.

"But I hate waiting," complained Tom.

"Well, that's just hard luck, then, isn't it?" Anna giggled, as she took Tom's arm.

They walked until they could hear only the ocean. Anna pointed at a black shadow in the distance, silhouetted against the moonlit ocean. "That," she said, "is Molokini. It's another small island."

She turned to face Tom and looked straight into his eyes. "It's so wonderful for me to show this to someone who has never seen it, and I am especially happy to be here with you, Tom." She put her arms around his neck and kissed him gently. He did not resist but instead held her close, giving into the wonderful feeling of holding her in his arms. They stood in silence for a few moments and listened to the waves breaking against the shore.

As they drove back to the house, Tom tried to make plans for the next day. "I must ring Bernard Lyle," he said, "he needs to get us some help to sort out the box."

"Wouldn't your Uncle Al know someone?" Anna asked.

"No," said Tom sharply, "definitely not!"

They took one last look at the ocean from the veranda before retiring to bed.

Tom woke to the chatter of birdsong and the sun bursting in through the windows. It was seven o'clock and the world was well and truly awake. The Clipper Room was incredible. The oak panels lining the walls and ceiling apparently came from the actual captain's cabin of a tea clipper, and all the furniture matched. Brass chronographs and barometers told you all you could ever want to know about time, the tide and the weather. The en suite bathroom was modern, with black and white marble tiles, a big roll top bath and a huge shower cabinet. The shower itself was fantastic and gave a full and hard spray that was wonderful to stand under. A bay window with French doors led out onto the balcony that ran around the house. Below, Tom could see the well-kept garden and just a glimpse of the sea through the trees. He was still gazing at the view when he heard footsteps behind him and turned to find Anna standing there. "Good morning," she said. She was wearing a white and blue kimono-style robe and her hair was still tousled from sleep. Even so, she was the most beautiful thing Tom had ever seen. "You're missing the best of the view," she said, "come this way."

Tom followed her around the balcony until it widened out in front of the master bedroom. A table and four chairs had been set out in front of the French windows on the balcony, along with a pot of coffee and two cups.

"Gosh," said Tom. "Bartholomew was up early!"

"No, that was me. I was awake at four and couldn't get back to sleep after that."

They drank coffee whilst looking out over the sea and planning their day. At ten, Tom rang Bernard Lyle at his home in London, where it was already eight in the evening. He said he would try and find someone to help with the box, but it could be difficult. Tom also told Bernard about his meetings in San Francisco and shared his discomfort about Chance Moxford. When Anna went for a shower, he decided to go for a walk. The sand was soft and heavy going and it seemed that just three houses shared the beach. As he drew parallel with the last one in the row, he heard a voice calling. A small woman in a wide-brimmed hat was waving. Tom walked towards her.

"Morning," she said, "I'm just letting you know that this is really a private beach."

"Oh, erm, I know," said Tom. "I'm staying at Ka'Lani."

"Oh, you are, huh? Then a very good morning and welcome – I'm Miriam Epstein." She held out her hand.

"Hello, Miriam, I'm Tom Dwyer."

The woman continued. "Well, it must be a couple of years since that place had visitors. Eighteen months at the very least. The family who own it don't come anymore, sadly."

"Well," said Tom, "Miss Aldridge is here now."

"Anna is here?" Miriam sounded delighted.

"Yes, she is – we arrived yesterday."

"Oh, that's fantastic! Please tell her I'm here – I would love to see her! She and I spent long holidays together here as kids."

"I'll tell her just as soon as I get back," promised Tom.

"You be sure to do that. Oh, and Tom?" He turned to look at her. "Tell her that 'they' are back."

Tom waved goodbye, managing not to show his frustration.

Back at the house, Bartholomew was setting out breakfast on the terrace. "Good morning, sir. If you don't mind me saying, bare feet are best for this beach – shoes make it very hard to walk."

Tom agreed with a smile and poured some coffee. He was back looking at the ocean and the empty beach when Anna appeared, once again looking radiant in a turquoise silk shirt hung loose over a white skirt.

"Wow, I never thought I would see this again," she said, as she took in the view.

"I've just met a friend of yours," Tom said. "She said to tell you 'they' are back."

Anna laughed again at Tom's obvious frustration. "Who was it?" she asked.

"I'll tell you if you tell me who 'they' are," he joked.

"I will take you to meet 'them' later. Now, who was it?"

"Miriam Epstein."

Anna's face lit up. "Miriam! Where is she? Is she at the house?"

Anna walked out onto the deck and looked down the beach. "Wow, I must call her. She and I were really good friends."

Breakfast was scrambled eggs and bacon and French toast and maple syrup, with pineapple to follow. Bartholomew was clearly no slouch in the kitchen.

"We need to go soon," said Anna, "and you need to change."

Tom looked shocked. "Why?" he asked.

"Because a jacket and a collar and tie will not work when we go to see 'them,'" she teased. "Shorts, a t-shirt and flip flops are more their thing."

Tom did as he was told, selecting a polo shirt, shorts and sandals from his wardrobe. Anna drove them to Lahaina, clearly enjoying keeping him in suspense. They walked along the dock and boarded a yellow inflatable Zodiac. A man greeted them and immediately started the outboard engine. They went slowly at first, but were soon flying along and bouncing over the waves, so they had to hold on tight. They approached the island that Anna had pointed out the previous evening and Tom assumed that must be where 'they' lived. But suddenly, the helmsman shut down the engines and let the boat drift.

"Look!" said Anna, as she pointed at a large, flat, black-and-white object that was slapping down on the surface of the water again and again. "'They' are here!"

At last Tom realised what was happening – whales! The whales were back!

"This is called pec slapping, Tom," Anna explained. "They slap their pectoral fins on the water to announce that they are there!"

Soon, and with a loud whoosh, a rolling black shape appeared and then disappeared with a flourish of its huge fluke. Tom was transfixed. Soon, there were four large creatures quite close to the small boat. Tom looked concerned.

"It's OK, they're fine," Anna reassured him. "They are just looking at us."

"But they're so big!" Tom said.

"Yes," agreed Anna. "They weigh around forty tons each. They're here for around four months, and in that time they don't eat a thing."

"What, nothing?"

"No, they eat krill, which lives in the colder waters of the north. They come here to have their young in these warmer waters and they feed them on their rich milk – somewhere around forty gallons a day – until they are strong enough to make the return trip."

"That's fantastic! I never dreamed of anything like this!"

They watched the pod for an hour or more, until they swam away.

"So, that's it," said Anna. "It's illegal to chase them – they must come to you, so we mustn't follow. Look!" She pointed as a green turtle surfaced and then paddled determinedly away from the boat before disappearing under water. "Oh, don't you just wish you could jump in and follow it," Anna said. "Have you ever been snorkelling?"

"No, but I used to swim a lot in the river."

"Well, that's definitely a trip for another day," said Anna. "There are some great spots here."

Chapter Seventeen

Clues and Crosswords

They cruised around and watched several more pods of whales before a school of spinner dolphins kept them entertained for a while longer. By now, it was getting very hot so they headed back to the dock and Anna drove them towards Ka'Lani. Before they got there, she pulled into a driveway Tom didn't recognise.

"Come on," she said. "Let's see if Miriam's in."

Luckily she was, and the two women almost turned cartwheels in the excitement of their reunion. They hugged, stood back and looked at each other, before hugging again. Miriam's house wasn't as big as Ka'Lani, but it was still quite grand.

"So, have you lived here long?" asked Tom.

"Well, sort of always really, on and off. It was my parents' summer home. They owned a department store in San Francisco and when they closed the business and retired they moved here. I came with them. They have both passed on now, so it's just me rattling around in this big old place, but I could never leave it."

"Miriam is a potter, Tom, she does some wonderful work," Anna explained. "Do you still do it, Mim?" she asked.

"Oh, yes, come and see." Miriam led them to the back garden of the house, where her workshop and kiln were situated. Her pots, plates, dishes and mugs were all decorated with native designs from all over the world. She explained that she sold mainly to the upper end of the tourist market and undertook special commissions. Besides her artistic skills, she was an expert on humpback whales and the house was full of pictures and statues of them. Tom liked Miriam a lot and felt sure she was to be trusted.

Anna invited Miriam to join them at Ka'Lani for dinner the following day, and she escorted them to the car to say goodbye. Something had been bothering Tom all day and he chose that moment to enquire further.

"Miriam, when we met this morning, you told me someone had stayed at Ka'Lani about eighteen months ago. Do you know who it was?"

"Uh, no, I don't, but ask Bartholomew – he won't forget that pair, I'm sure."

"Pair?" Tom enquired.

"Yes, a very pushy man – full of himself if you ask me – and his cow of a wife! They treated Mariah like dirt, all because she didn't have a safe for the cow to keep her jewellery in."

"OK, thanks," said Tom. "I'll ask Bartholomew."

As they drove away, Anna asked, "Are you thinking what I'm thinking?"

"I probably am, but let's see what Bartholomew has to say." Tom was clearly not going to let this drop.

"Let me speak to him," Anna said.

"OK, but let's do it now."

When they got in, Anna asked Bartholomew for a rum and coke with ice and asked if he could please bring out three glasses. Very soon, a tray with a bottle of Mount Gay rum, some small cans of coke and an ice bucket were set out on the veranda.

"Bartholomew, will you join us in a glass? I know you love it!" said Anna.

"Well, uh, yes, ma'am. Thank you, that would be really fine. It comes from my island, you know!" Bartholomew was clearly proud of his Barbadian roots.

Anna poured him a large measure. "It's OK, you can sit down," she said, offering him a chair. Now he looked worried.

"Nothing's wrong," Anna reassured him. "We'd just like to know who else has stayed here over the last year or two?"

"Oh, sure," he said, looking pleased. "I thought old Bartholomew was out of work there for a minute. Well, miss, not many people have been here since Miss Emily passed on. Sometimes she would send people – real fine people, good folk. Since then, Mr Moxford has come twice. He was OK, but he didn't want Mariah or me here. He sent us home and took care of himself. He moved a lot of the furniture around, though.

"Al Dwyer from San Francisco came twice. He was a very quiet man and he also didn't want us here. I don't think he wanted to be any trouble, but he also moved stuff around in almost every room.

"The last lot were Mr and Mrs De Vere. That's another story. Mr De Vere asked lots of questions about when I came here, and about Mr Victor. He wanted to know if he ever told me secrets about his business. He said he was writing a book about him and wanted to find any old papers that might be hidden away. He even offered me two hundred dollars to tell. I told him I didn't know nothing and he got real mad and called me a stupid, dirty nigger."

Anna gasped.

"Well, ma'am, that didn't really bother me none. Old Bartholomew has been called worse than that, and it didn't hurt. It just makes the folks who say it look stupid."

"What about Mrs De Vere?" Anna asked, topping up Bartholomew's glass.

"Well, ma'am, she was bad news. She got real bad with drink and would shout and cuss at Mariah and me. The worst was when she wanted to lock her jewellery in the safe. Mariah told her there wasn't one here and she accused her of lying. She said she knew Mr Victor had one. In the end, she claimed that Mariah just wanted to steal her rings and stuff, and she said she knew what thieving blacks were like. When Mariah came and told me, I called Mr Dwyer in San Francisco and he said he would sort it out. A few days later, they left and Mr Victor sent us two hundred dollars each and told us to forget it. Have I done wrong, ma'am?"

"No, Bartholomew. You are a good man and you'll have a place here just as long as you want it."

Bartholomew smiled his toothy grin and sipped his rum.

"Just one last thing," said Tom. "This Mr De Vere – what did he look like?"

"Well, sir, he wasn't quite as tall as you, but he was about the same age. He had short hair, dark-rimmed glasses and wore very smart, expensive clothes."

Anna and Tom exchanged glances; they both knew Dyson's trademarks.

"So, tell me more about this island of yours, Bartholomew," said Tom, lightening the conversation and bringing a beam to Bartholomew's face, as he recounted his life story. He and his brother had worked for Victor Margesson as cane cutters on a sugar plantation in Barbados and other islands. He also cooked, and Victor enjoyed his meals so much that when he moved to Maui to manage the coffee plantation, he asked Bartholomew to go with him. "So here I was just 18 years old and cooking for people in this wonderful house. I only had my mama's recipes, but I learned more from other people here. It was a busy house then – lots of staff."

"What about your brother?" asked Tom.

"He went to England with his wife and young baby – they lived in London. It was hard at first, but he did OK. He is an old man now, like me. He was a builder and had his own business, but he is retired now and his daughter is a doctor."

"Have you seen your brother lately?" asked Tom.

"Oh no, sir, we write regularly, though. I've only seen him once in all this time, and that was when Mama died." Bartholomew was filling up with tears. "We both went home then, sir."

Anna gave him the rest of the day off and she and Tom remained on the veranda. As they sat watching the daylight fade, Anna explained that Bartholomew and Mariah had been together for many years, but had never married.

"So," she said. "Alex Dyson has been here, then." Once again, she was showing signs of her hurt and anger. "And who was the woman?" she added.

"Well," said Tom, "of course we now know he's not Dyson at all – he's Timothy Welland."

"Agreed," said Anna, "but he will always be Alex Dyson to me."

"Me too," said Tom. "There's no doubt in my mind that he's been here, and I think I now know how he knew about the money."

"Really, how?"

"Well, either via Chance Moxford or Uncle Al. Someone in that crew must have signed the money off when I asked for it – that was the only cash I could access quickly."

"Oh, my goodness, you're right. We can't trust them either."

"Don't worry," said Tom. "I'm not going to."

The wind picked up and the temperature went down. Anna lit the fire that was set in the drawing room. Bartholomew had left them fresh crab and salad for dinner, along with key lime pie for dessert – another monumental culinary success. They ate in the kitchen, as the dining room was too cold and formal. After dinner, they returned to the drawing room and put extra logs on the fire. Anna poured more rum and they sat in the firelight as the wind rattled the shutters outside.

"Tom, I'm scared," Anna confessed. "This whole business is getting worse. Something really bad is going on here. I've been so stupid letting that bloody man walk all over me while being convinced he loved me – I'm just a stupid little girl. No wonder you're not interested in me."

They were silent for an awkward few moments until Anna got up. "I'm going to bed. I'm sorry, Tom, I've embarrassed you. I'm just making matters worse."

"No, don't go, please. Come and sit here." He took her hand and she sat beside him on the couch. "Is that what you really think? That I'm not interested in you?"

"I'm sorry, I know you're a good friend to me, but..."

"That's not what I meant," Tom said. "Listen, I feel so much for you that I'm almost bursting. I think you're probably the most beautiful woman I've ever met – far too beautiful to be interested in the likes of me. When we talked in San Francisco, I told you I was worried about us getting too close. Well, that was true. You're very hurt and vulnerable at the moment and I don't want to take advantage of that. Also, from a selfish point of view, I don't want to be hurt when things get sorted out and you go off with someone else. I don't do love by halves – no one night stands or 'it was fun for a while and goodbye' for me. It's all or nothing. I did it once and I was left with nothing except hurt. I won't pay that price again, for anything or anyone, but I will take care of you and protect you until ... until..."

"Until what, Tom? Until some knight rides up on a charger to whisk me away to his castle? Oh, and then you can go and lick your wounds and say, 'I knew that would happen'? Well, I really don't understand you, Tom – you trust me enough to give me large sums of money, but you don't trust me when I say I love you!"

Anna was getting louder and angrier. Tom stared into the fire for several minutes before breaking the silence. "But you've never said that."

"Maybe not in so many words, but surely I've given you a few clues?"

"Clues? It's not a bloody crossword!"

Anna giggled. "I don't know, you sound pretty cross to me!"

Tom had to smile and his anger melted away.

"OK, here it is. I think I love you, Tom Dwyer. Will that do it?"

Tom took her in his arms. "Well, it will certainly do for a start," he said.

They kissed in the firelight, but the moment was shattered by the phone's shrill ring. Bernard Lyle had found a contact at the Polynesian Investment Corporation. "She'll be with you tomorrow," he told Tom. "Her name is Myra Rea – she will call you on your mobile from the airport."

"OK, thanks, that's great," said Tom. He then shared his suspicions that Moxford and Al Dwyer were mixed up with Dyson.

"At the moment, let's keep them out of everything bar essential business," Bernard Lyle agreed.

Once the phone call was over, Tom hugged Anna again. "Look, now we know where we both stand, let's just take it slowly, for each other's sake. But I do love you, too. For now, we have our work cut out trying to get to the bottom of what's going on."

"Well, it's pretty clear that they all came here looking for something – documents of some kind – and it sounds like they didn't find what they were looking for."

Tom nodded. "I think the stuff about the safe was a ploy to find out if there was one."

"Yes, the even stranger thing is that there is, or at least there was."

"Do you know where?"

"Well, let's see."

Anna took off up the stairs, with Tom close behind. The lights in the Clipper Room were on a dimmer switch, which needed to be turned up full to give any clarity.

"Give me a hand to move this desk, will you," Anna said.

They moved the large partner desk a few feet away

from the wall and then Anna pushed the oak panel in and sideways to reveal the English-made Tann safe. "It needs a key and a combination, and we don't have either," she said, defeated.

"I'm sure there's a key in the box at the bank," said Tom, "otherwise, we'll just have to get a locksmith."

Tom's cold logic made it all sound very simple. They replaced the panel and the desk, kissed once more and bade each other goodnight.

Tom slept better than he had done for months and didn't wake until eight-thirty. The weather was horrid. The palm trees were bending in the wind and the rain was driving into the windows on the ocean side of the house. Anna was already up and was busy writing postcards to Helen and CJ. "Ah, good morning, sleepyhead," she said.

"I know," said Tom. "I don't know what happened – I haven't slept like that for months – years even!"

Anna put toast and an egg in front of him and whispered, "It must be the love of a good woman."

They both giggled and Bartholomew looked puzzled as he poured their coffee.

Myra Rea rang to say that she was at the airport and would not be going back to the big island any time soon. "After a flight like that I'm keeping both feet on the ground until this storm has played out," she said.

They agreed to meet her at the bank at eleven. In the meantime, they would book her into the Maui Sheraton.

Myra Rea was a force to be reckoned with. She was five foot ten tall, with blond hair almost down to her waist, long legs and a short shirt. She spoke with a Southern drawl and didn't take any prisoners. In no time at all, she had the bank staff eating out of her hand.

She carefully listed the share certificates and faxed them to her office for valuation, before sorting the property titles into commercial, domestic and development.

"I can tell you now that some of these shares are real peaches. Most are pretty good and there are only a few dogs," she said, bringing the whole business down to brass tacks. "Our property guys will take a day or two to weigh up the land and property, but it looks like a really nice portfolio to me. Boy, I wish I'd been shrewd enough to buy like that!"

Tom and Anna sorted out the rest of the contents of the box, mainly jewellery and trinkets, and of the two keys they took, one looked like a very likely candidate for the safe. They delivered Myra Rea to the hotel and drove home through the howling storm. Once inside, they rushed to the Clipper Room, pulled back the desk, slid back the panel and tried the key. It turned, but without the combination, the safe wouldn't open.

Chapter Eighteen

Dinner and Diamonds

Several times that afternoon, they dragged the desk and slid the panel, as Anna came up with different combinations made up of family birthdays and telephone numbers.

Bartholomew served tea and what he called biscuits, but Tom called scones. He glanced at the key on the table and turned to Anna. "Miss, if you're missing any numbers, you could try 20-11-50; Mr Victor used that for everything. It was the date of his wedding to Miss Emily."

Tom and Anna looked at each other in amazement.

"Bartholomew – did you know where the safe was?" Anna asked.

"Why, yes!"

"And you didn't tell?"

"Why, no, miss."

"Even when Mr and Mrs De Vere were pressing you?"

"No, because Mr Victor told me not to tell."

Anna shook her head. "Bartholomew, you are one in a million."

"Yes, miss," he replied, flashing his toothy smile and leaving the room.

They both flew up the stairs and pressed 20-11-50 – the handle turned. Inside the safe was a pair of pistols in an oak box, ammunition, money in several different currencies, some of which were now defunct, a box containing a necklace of pink diamonds and two envelopes – one filled to the brim with papers and one containing old photographs, mainly of the coffee plantation and the roasting and packing plant, which probably dated from the late 40s or 50s. Tom found them fascinating. The papers mostly related to two properties – one in Nevada that seemed to be a casino and the title deeds to land on the Big Island in Hawaii. They were tightly tied with green ribbon.

Tom took one of the pistols from its box. "These need to be looked at," he said.

"Put it away, Tom, it makes me shiver," Anna pleaded. Then she added: "Hey, look, a dinner menu from their wedding!" She held it out for Tom to see, before following it up with, "Oh, shit! Dinner, Miriam! I clean forgot. We'll just have to go out."

They packed everything back in the safe before showering, changing and arriving downstairs just as Miriam knocked on the door. They drove to the Hilo Bisto and were able to get a table despite it being so busy. The food was good; Anna and Miriam opted for the chilli con carne and Tom decided to stick with fish. As they ate, Anna and Miriam brought each other up to speed with their lives – almost. Anna didn't say anything about the Dyson saga.

"So, how long have you two been an item?" Miriam asked. "It seems like you've been together for years!"

"We've only known each other for a short time," said

Tom, trying his best to be honest without admitting to anything. But Miriam was in full flight, which may have been something to do with the three margaritas she'd polished off in quick succession. "Goodness, you must be bored, Tom, listening to two girls recount their life stories." She signalled to the waiter for refills.

"Not at all. How could I be bored in the company of two beautiful women?"

"Anna, I love this man! Keep hold of him. Good ones are hard to find. I should know, I've checked lots of oysters and haven't yet found a pearl."

Anna, who had matched Miriam drink for drink, was very quiet and simply smiled a lot.

After their meal, they dropped Miriam home and Tom helped Anna up the stairs at Ka'Lani. He sat on the bed and kissed her goodnight.

"Don't go," she said, "stay with me."

"What!" he said, "you mean take advantage of a lady worse for drink? That wouldn't be very gallant." He kissed her again. "See you in the morning," he said.

It felt as if he'd hardly been asleep when the sound of Bartholomew shouting woke him up. "Help, Mr Tom, help!"

He rushed downstairs to find Bartholomew bleeding from the head. "There was a man, sir, in the sitting room – he was taking your briefcase. I called 911, but he heard me and knocked me down. I grabbed his leg and he fell, and I managed to hit him, but he was too strong for me. I told him I'd called 911 and he ran out of the back door. He did drop the case, though, sir, it's here."

After taking the case, Tom turned on his heels and flew up the stairs to Anna's room. She was still dressed, but sleeping like a baby on top of the bed. By the time he returned to Bartholomew's side, a black and white police car was at the front door, with all its lights flashing. The officer was thorough and deliberate in his enquiries and Bartholomew gave the best description he could provide, giving details of a tall, thin man in motorcycle clothes, including a helmet and gloves.

Tom tried to explain his concerns about Dyson, but the young officer showed no signs of taking them in.

"I see this kind of thing several times every couple of weeks," he said. "Youngsters break into houses they think are empty and then panic and run when they discover they aren't. Most are too scared to go back again."

Bartholomew's head had stopped bleeding and he refused further treatment. The officer's colleague searched the grounds, but no more could be done.

"Are you OK?" Tom asked Bartholomew, as the police car drove away.

"Yes, sir, I'm just mad about being so old and slow. A few years ago, I would have had him pinned down and wrapped in ribbon for you. But I do know one thing – the intruder was no kid."

"I know," said Tom, "I know." He went back to the Clipper Room and returned with the pistols.

"Do you know how to use one of these?" he asked Bartholomew.

"Err, yes, sir."

Tom watched as Bartholomew cleaned and loaded each gun.

"OK, you keep one and I'll take the other, but we say nothing about these to Miss Anna."

Bartholomew agreed and took his pistol to his room. Tom placed his under his mattress in the Clipper Room. He cleared up and made coffee, as the birds burst into song. Anna appeared at almost 9 o'clock. Contrary to how Tom thought she would be, she was bouncing with life.

"Well, that was a bit of a night, wasn't it? I'm afraid I went at it a bit too hard, but thanks for taking care of me." She scrutinised Tom's face. "Well, that's a bit unfair," she said. "I'm the one who did the drinking and you look like you're the one with the hangover!"

"Anna, sit down and listen." She detected the serious tone and did as he said. "We had a break in last night. Bartholomew was attacked, but he's OK. The police say it's kids, but I'm not convinced. Although the description didn't match Alex, I believe it could be someone acting for him. They were after my briefcase. It's possible they have been watching us and know we went to the bank."

The glow had gone from Anna's cheeks. "So, what do we do?"

"Well, first and foremost, we must stay together at all times. I have a plan to draw whoever this is into the open. We need some help and Miriam might have a good contact, but you'll need to tell her everything. Also, you and I need to take a trip into town."

"OK," Anna agreed.

Tom made a call and left a message for Detective Superintendent Marsden back in the UK. Later, they met once more with Myra Rea before she left the island. Tom handed over the papers from the small safe, having had the bank make copies, and he also faxed a list of requests to Bernard Lyle in London.

"Somewhere in among the paperwork you have a deal

that is causing someone some discomfort," Tom explained. "I'd like to know what this is, and to whom. There are the deeds to a casino in there – it could be that."

"OK," said Myra. "I'll give it my best shot."

Next, they drove to Miriam's house and found her loading a kiln in the workshop. Anna brought her up to speed and finished with an account of the break in. When she'd finished, Miriam précised the whole thing. "Well, sounds like you found yourself a pedigree dirtbag there!"

"No doubt about that," said Anna.

"Now," said Tom, "after what happened last night I want to try and force these people into the open. Miriam, we need your help. Do you know anyone in the press who could quickly run a story?"

"Possibly," said Miriam. "I'll call them."

Within an hour, Miriam's journalist friend Bob was interviewing Anna. Photographs were taken and in no time at all Bob was hightailing the article back to the office to try and catch the close deadline. The story was on its way to press faster than Tom could have ever imagined. It seemed that in the scheme of things for this place, either it was a big story or there wasn't much else happening. Anna had talked about returning to Maui for the first time since the death of her grandmother some years ago, and how the trip had brought back many happy memories. She added how she had also found lost photographs and documents secretly stored by her grandfather. These included photos of an old coffee plantation and packaging plant, as well as some important and valuable property papers that had been missing for a long time. Anna spoke of her intention to donate the photographs to the local museum and the newspaper agreed to publish some of them over the coming weeks, as they included many employees who the island's residents would recognise.

The following day, Anna took Tom on another sightseeing trip and they visited more places that she remembered from her childhood. Afterwards, they went to see Miriam to thank her for her help with getting the press coverage. The morning paper had hit centre target with the secondary headline, *Heiress Returns to Maui and has a Lucky Find*. A photo of Anna topped off the piece, along with a small picture of a group of workers at the factory, which was offered as a taster of what was to come.

"Well, I'm glad it worked," said Miriam. "But for heaven's sake be careful."

Tom nodded. "There's a way to go yet but thanks for a good start," he said. "Let's see if they take the bait."

Anna invited Miriam to dinner again and promised that it would be the full Bartholomew speciality this time. Tom decided to leave the two women together and return to the house. Anna asked him to inform Bartholomew there would be three for dinner at seven. "Tell him to do something special. We'll be back by then, promise," she said.

Tom took the short walk back to Ka'Lani and delivered Anna's message to Bartholomew, who looked delighted at the challenge. "I have some calls to make," Tom added, "but let's have a glass of rum together in an hour."

"Yes, sir," Bartholomew said with great excitement. "I will set it out on the veranda."

It was now 3:30 in the afternoon, Tom phoned Bernard Lyle, who had stayed up especially to speak to him.

"I have done the things you asked, Tom," he said. "First of all, I spoke to Detective Superintendent Marsden. She is going to call you shortly. She's worried and wants me to impress on you that you must not go it alone. She's been trying to speak to the local police in Maui. I'm sure she will fill you in."

"Yes, that's what I was hoping. I need their help on this," said Tom.

Bernard continued. "As you requested, I have also spoken to Myra Rea. Her people have looked at the papers you gave her and there is one that leaps out as hot."

"I guess that's the casino," said Tom.

"No, it's a plot of land on the Big Island. Apparently, developers have been trying to get their hands on it for decades. Many years ago, Victor and Emily refused to sell, as they believed it was a good investment holding. Recently, the developers employed agents to track down the ownership and there is a bounty of one million dollars for whoever brings the deal home."

"The HANA Trust could find no record of it, so Victor Margesson must have held onto it personally. The developers who want to get their hands on the plot are called Meridian Developments Hawaii – MDH. I looked into them. Guess who is on their board? Mr A Dwyer and Mr C Moxford. Just be careful, Tom, MDH have a reputation for playing dirty."

"Well, there's our answer," said Tom. "All I need to know now is where Dyson fits into all this. I am beginning to think I know."

As he rang off, his head was spinning with the implications. He took a copy of the morning paper out onto the veranda to show Bartholomew, and, after pouring out two large glasses of Mount Gay, he explained what he had done and how he expected someone to return to try and get their hands on what they had failed to when they broke in. "This time, we will be ready for them," he said. "I'm trying to get help from the police and we will need to keep watch through the night."

Bartholomew was more than willing to help protect Miss Anna and agreed to Tom's plan without question.

A few minutes later, the phone rang. It was Detective Superintendent Marsden. "Are you and Anna OK?" she asked. When Tom confirmed they were, she continued. "Listen, you must not take this man on. This is a job for the police. We now have a lot more information about Dyson, also known as Timothy John Welland, and he's dangerous. The Maui police were reluctant to wade in but I think I got them to see the seriousness of the situation. You need to speak to Lieutenant Chang, as he is now fully briefed. Promise me you'll do that, Mr Dwyer?"

Tom agreed. "I will do it immediately. So, you obviously think Dyson is behind all this, then?"

"Well, I can tell you that one of his alias passports went through Manchester Airport, bound stateside, about a week ago. Unfortunately, it was before our marker went live, but it does mean that he is probably in the States. Speak to Lieutenant Chang and stay close together."

"OK," said Tom. "I understand."

He immediately rang the number Detective Superintendent Marsden had given him and was promised a call back as soon as Chang returned to the office. He then went back onto the veranda so he and Bartholomew could finish their planning. The two men finished their rum in the last rays of the afternoon's daylight. They weren't expecting their enemy's next move to come quite so soon.

In the comfort of Miriam's sitting room, the two old friends were deep in conversation and hadn't noticed the time ticking by.

"My goodness," said Miriam, looking at her watch. "We should go soon." She went off to change and Anna looked around the neat sitting room, admiring some of the books and paintings until a sound outside resembling a load of bottles being tipped and smashed startled her. She looked out of the window and saw Miriam going into her workshop. As she crossed the lawn, she called out "Mim," but there was no reply. She pushed open the workshop door and could see that the floor was covered in broken pottery. "Oh no, what happened?" she called out, but as she looked up she could see exactly what had just taken place. Miriam was sitting in a chair, stiff with terror. A thin, wispy figure wearing motorcycle leathers and a Bell helmet stood over her. He was clutching a baseball bat.

"Who are you? What do you want?" As Anna spoke, a voice behind her doubled her level of fear to the point where she felt almost paralysed.

"Hello, darling. Well, isn't this nice?"

Anna turned to see Alex pointing a gun straight at her. Terror took hold, but at the same time came a rising anger and hatred of this man for what he had done to her, which made her want to lash out and hurt him. "What do you want?" she said, spitting out the words with venom.

"Now, don't be like that," Alex said. "It's all very simple, you see. I think you and your little farmer playmate have got something I need. Just one little thing out of all that you have. That's not too much, is it?"

Dyson's patronising tone was making Anna even angrier.

"Now, if you just hand over what I want, we can do this real easy," Dyson added.

"I don't see why I should, but what is it you're so interested in?"

"I'm working for some people who would really like the deeds to a property on the Big Island. I think you have them. If you could just hand them over, we'll get the transfer document signed and me and Marky will be on our way. You'll never see us again. Now, where are they?"

"I don't know what you are talking about, but all the papers are with the bank," Anna said.

"OK, so we'll see if our friendly farmer knows where they are."

He took out his mobile phone and dialled.

Back at the house, Tom was beginning to wonder where Anna and Miriam were. As the phone rang, Bartholomew was rushing back and forth laying the table and Tom picked it up before he could get to it. "Ka'Lani?" he said.

"Well, hello, Mr Thomas Dwyer! Now, you weren't expecting to hear from me, were you?"

Tom instantly knew who it was. "What do you want?" he said.

"Well, we have some business to do. You see, you have something I want and I seem to have something of yours. I'm proposing a little trade."

"I want nothing to do with you! The police are hunting you down," said Tom.

"Oh, is that right?" Dyson's tone was deliberately arrogant. Tom heard him speak to someone else. "He does not seem to think you're worth it, darling."

Tom heard Anna scream at Dyson to leave her alone. "If you so much as touch a hair on her head, so help me I will kill you," he said firmly. He felt cold to the pit of his stomach, but he knew he had to keep Dyson engaged.

"OK, what do you want? But don't hurt her." He tried not to sound like he was pleading, but he was.

"You have the deeds to a plot of land on the Big Island and you need to bring them here so we can sign them over. Then we can all go home, providing you don't try anything silly and involve the police further."

"Where are you?" said Tom. "Where's Anna?"

Feeling he now had the upper hand, Dyson said, "Have you got what I want?"

"Yes, I think so. Now, where is Anna?" said Tom, knowing full well that he didn't actually have the document – it had gone with Myra Rea.

"Don't you worry, I have someone taking good care of her and her little friend. You just concentrate on getting me what I want and don't do anything silly. No police, or I promise you will regret it."

Tom heard the clear threat from Dyson. "What do you want me to do?" he asked.

"Just bring the document to the potter's workshop, without speaking to anyone else. If you do as I say you will all leave safely, but one wrong move and someone will get hurt."

Dyson's menacing tone once again made Tom feel cold. He had heard the threats before but this time he sounded desperate as he said, "I'm on my way. Don't hurt anyone."

The line went dead.

Chapter Nineteen

Risking it All

Tom quickly filled Bartholomew in and told him to call Lieutenant Chang straightaway, but to impress on him Dyson's threat. "He must be careful," he urged.

He was shaking as he placed a photocopy of the document into an envelope. He was not yet ready for this, it had all happened too soon. He went to the Clipper Room and pulled out the pistol from under the mattress.

Some lights were on at Miriam's house, but Tom went straight round the back and across the lawn. The workshop lights were on and a figure was standing outside the door. Tom could make out Dyson's shape in the half-light. "Have you got it?" he asked.

"Yes," Tom replied.

By now he could see a pistol pointing straight at him. Dyson flicked the weapon towards the door and ordered, "Get inside."

Tom did as instructed. Within the potter's workshop, Anna was handcuffed to a central iron column that supported the roof. Miriam was still seated, but the thin man, Marky, was leaning against a wall nearby, brandishing a baseball bat.

Tom handed Dyson the envelope that contained the copy of the deed and held his breath as he looked at it. To Tom's immense relief, he made no comment. "What now?" he asked.

"Now we wait," said Dyson. He took his mobile phone out of his pocket and dialled a number. "It's me, I have what you want. Yes, he's here and he'll sign. Do you have the cash? OK, I'm at the potter's house I told you about and we are at the back, in the workshop. Make sure no one follows you." Dyson rang off.

"This will never stand up legally," said Anna. "You'll never get away with it."

"I don't give a damn, darling! I will be long gone," Dyson gloated.

Meanwhile, Miriam was shuffling around on her chair and sliding it sideways. "I need to pee," she said.

Marky straightened up and stood over her. "Well, that's just tough shit," he said, waving the bat in her face.

After a short while, footsteps sounded outside. Dyson opened the door and two men stepped in. A younger man, who Tom guessed was in his 20s, was carrying a leather holdall. Tom had met the older man just a few days earlier – it was Chance Moxford from San Francisco. Ignoring everyone else, he looked straight at Dyson. "Where is it?" he asked.

But before Dyson could speak, the younger man interrupted. "Dad, for God's sake, what's going on here?" He was clearly shocked by the sight of the guns and the hostages.

"Shut it!" Moxford said. "Sometimes, you've gotta get tough to get business done, right?" He waited for an answer but none was forthcoming. "Right?" he asked again.

"OK," the young man relented.

Moxford continued. "Let's see what you've got," he said.

"Let me see the money first," Dyson insisted. The younger man opened the bag to reveal bundles of dollar bills. Dyson handed over the envelope and Chance Moxford looked inside it. Tom held his breath.

"This is a copy! Where's the original?" Moxford said, looking at Dyson accusingly.

"It's all we have," Tom responded.

Once again, Miriam shuffled sideways on the chair, causing Marky to strike her across the face with his hand and order her to sit still. But at last her arm could reach. Stretching out, she pulled hard on the handle of the kiln, falling backwards as it flung open. The surge of heat sent Marky flying sideways. Tom took the pistol from his pocket, aimed at Dyson and fired. But, not used to handling guns, the recoil spoiled his aim and the shot went high. As he fell to the floor, he felt a thud and a burning pain in his chest. After that, he couldn't hear much except Anna in the distance, yelling, "Tom! No, nooooo!"

He saw several more flashes and then darkness closed over him.

Chapter Twenty

End Game

Anna sat on the veranda and watched the sun rise over Ka'Lani. The dawn chorus was in full swing, almost to a deafening level, and the sea gently lapped small waves onto the sand. She had not slept; instead she had gone over and over the implications of what had just happened. It had been five days since the incident, and she had spent five nights alone at Ka'Lani reflecting on her life. They were five of the loneliest nights she had ever known. She wanted so much for her life to be stable and to share it with someone else. On a few occasions in recent weeks, she had seen glimpses of what that could feel like. Tom was so different. He understood and cared about her unconditionally, in a way she had never known before, but those moments had been short lived.

At 8 o'clock, Mariah arrived and made her breakfast.

"Join me for some coffee first?" Anna asked, and the two women sat looking at the ocean.

"Thank God for this peace, miss," Mariah said as she poured Anna yet another mug from the fresh pot. Anna nodded her agreement and smiled.

"I guess that will stop today when those two men come home," she added with a hearty laugh.

"I do hope so," said Anna. "I do hope so."

Tom was brought to Ka'Lani by ambulance and Bartholomew arrived by taxi, as he was fully mobile. Although still quite weak, Tom looked better than he had done for days. The bullet he took from Dyson had gone straight through his upper left chest, puncturing a lung on the way. Bartholomew, who'd arrived at Miriam's seconds after Tom had been shot, suffered a blow to the side of his head as Marky tried to leave in a hurry and cleared him from the path using the baseball bat. As he ran, brave Bartholomew had managed to shoot him in the leg.

Just after Tom arrived home, Lieutenant Chang turned up to bring everyone up to speed. "I am sorry I haven't been in touch," he said, "but I was off the job for a few days whilst internal affairs looked into the shooting. They now say it was clean so I am back on the streets."

Chang and two other officers had arrived at the workshop at the same time as Bartholomew. As Tom fell, Dyson turned his gun on Anna.

The police moved in and Chang took Dyson down with a clean shot to the head, killing him outright. The man with at least three identities – Timothy John Welland, Marcus Hodge and Alex Dyson – was now dead. The other officers apprehended Moxford and his son, who, in their panic, remained stock still with their hands raised waiting to be arrested.

Chang told them how the police had since apprehended Marky. He had fled back to his home in Honolulu, but had eventually gone to hospital to get treatment for his leg wound, as well as the burns to his hands and face sustained while trying to close the kiln door. The Honolulu police department picked him up there.

Chang continued. "Chance Moxford has been arraigned and is being held in custody pending trial. His son has not yet been charged, but that could happen later. How is Ms Epstein?"

Anna smiled as she answered. "She is good, thank you. She's been staying with friends on the other side of the island, but she's returning home tomorrow. She will be so pleased that you have Marky."

"I think it's best you have him for his own safety," Tom couldn't resist adding, "because if Miriam gets hold of him all bets are off."

Chang informed them that broader enquiries were now underway into the activities of Meridian Developments Hawaii, and two other directors had been arrested on charges of fraud and conspiracy. One of them was Mr Albert Dwyer of Sausalito, California. Chang asked Tom if it was any relation.

"Distant," Tom replied. "Very distant."

Chang continued. "There is one person we are still keen to speak to. Her name is Anita Williams, sometimes Harris, sometimes De Vere. Do you know anything about her?"

Tom and Anna nodded and told Chang about the De Vere's stay at Ka'Lani. Bartholomew gave his account and he also confirmed that Dyson was Mr De Vere.

After everyone had left, Tom and Anna sat on the veranda holding hands. Anna felt more relaxed than she had done in years and Tom was experiencing inner peace for the first time ever.

"So, now it's all over," Anna said. "We can just be ourselves."

"We can," Tom agreed, "but I think I'm still learning what that means."

Over the next few days, Tom recuperated from his injury and Anna continued to reform her close friendship with Miriam. They all spent a lot of time together, sightseeing and eating Bartholomew's wonderful food. A few days before they were due to leave, Anna threw a special dinner party. This time caterers were brought in because Bartholomew and Mariah were the guests of honour.

After dessert, Tom raised his glass. "We want to thank you both for all that you have been and all that you are," he said. "I especially want to thank you, Bartholomew, for being my friend and taking the risks with me. That's the mark of a true friend. He handed them an envelope, which Mariah took. When she saw what was inside, tears filled her eyes and she passed it to Bartholomew. Anna and Tom had paid for two business class seats to London and a month's stay at a hotel.

"You have to see your brother," said Tom, "and when you have done that you must come and see us."

The old man cried, unable to speak.

"We don't know what to say, you will never know how much this means to us," Mariah said.

On their final day before flying home, Tom, Anna and Miriam took a trip to see the whales. Many more had arrived in the bay since they last saw them, and the spectacle was amazing.

By now, it was completely clear to Miriam that her friend was madly in love, and she was pleased to see her so happy, even though it left her with her own pangs of loneliness.

Meanwhile, Tom and Anna knew there were going to be many more trips to paradise. They spent the evening on the veranda, enjoying the balmy evening air, the sound of the ocean and each other's company.

Anna tried to broach the subject of what would happen when they got home, knowing full well that Tom's caution would still be an issue. "What happens next?" she said bluntly.

"Ah, yes, I have been wondering about that, too. In fact, I have been thinking about it a lot."

"So?" said Anna. "What did you come up with?"

"Well, it all depends on what you want really."

"Oh, does it? So if I just want to go home and pretend that we don't have any feelings for each other and never have, that's OK, is it?"

"Well, that might be what you want," Tom said.

"Oh, for God's sake, Tom Dwyer!" Anna was exasperated, but nevertheless she threw her arms around Tom, held him close and stared right into his face. "I love you and I can tell you love me. So just stop trying to give me chances to walk away, because I am not going to. I thought for a moment recently that I had lost you, and that was unbearable."

The feeling of inner peace was just starting to become familiar to Tom, and as he felt it once more he kissed Anna passionately.

After they drew apart, they finished their drinks and went up to bed.

The following morning, the world was a new place. Tom and Anna held each other close and faced up to the fact that today they were going home.

"Will you come and stay with me at Larkspur?" Anna asked.

"Hmmm, well, I thought you might like to come and stay at the cottage?" said Tom, with his tongue firmly in his cheek.

"OK, as long as you are there, that's enough for me, but Larkspur does have hot water!" Anna replied with a smile.

"I want to tell Jack and Laura about us first," Tom said. "Then we should inform Helen and CJ, rather than just letting them find out." Tom had clearly worked this all out in his head already.

"I agree," Anna said, "but let's take a couple of days for us first. I just want us to be together."

Their flight was not until late afternoon, and Tom had one final task to do for the day. He sat at the desk in the sitting room and carefully dialled a telephone number.

"Castillion?"

"Could I speak to Mrs Dwyer please?"

"I'm afraid she's not here at the moment. She will be back in a couple of days. Can I say who called?"

Tom hesitated before replying. "Yes, please tell her that her son called and he will try again."

"Certainly, I will do that."

Tom knew that it wasn't going to be easy to build a relationship with his mother, especially as Al Dwyer was now being indicted for fraud, but he would keep working at it.

When they arrived back in England, the green fields that they had left behind in Oxfordshire had changed. A darker shade of green showed clear in the woodlands and hedgerows, as the conifers and other evergreens now dominated the view, and the deciduous trees stood gaunt and bare. The fields had been ploughed to a beautiful, rich brown and were waiting patiently for the seeds beneath them to bring forth new life in the spring. The almost-white sunlight, smoky chimneys, extra woollies and very early evenings meant that the world was settling in for the winter. For all of its stark contrast with the Hawaiian climate, Tom and Anna were happy with it; somehow this world fitted them with all of the warmth and comfort of an old shoe.

Acknowledgements

With sincere thanks to my friends for their encouragement and support, especially Christine for her work transcribing my manuscript, and Sally for her interest and encouragement to get it finished.

About the Author

Dave Webber retired from his job as the chief executive of an international charity in 2018, which gave him more time to dedicate to writing. He is also a singer-songwriter and regularly tours the UK and USA with his wife Anni Fentiman. Together they perform traditional folk music and have recorded six albums.

When he's not writing or singing, Dave enjoys bird watching in the Wiltshire countryside and spending time with his Burmese cats, Lily and Elsa. *A Secret Harvest* is his debut novel.